W9-AYI-039

RISK
N'
ROSES

ALSO BY JAN SLEPIAN:

The Broccoli Tapes

JAN SLEPIAN

AN
APPLE
PAPERBACK

SCHOLASTIC INC.
New York Toronto London Auckland Sydney

ISBN 0-590-45361-0

 Published by Scholastic Inc., 730 Broadway, New York, NY 10003, by arrangement with Philomel Books, a division of The Putnam & Grosset Book Group. APPLE PAPERBACKS is a registered trademark of Scholastic Inc.

12 11 10 9 8 7 6 5 4 3 2 1 2 3 4 5 6 7/9

Printed in the U.S.A. 28

First Scholastic printing, August 1992

To Patricia Lee Gauch: my friend, my editor, my pilot.

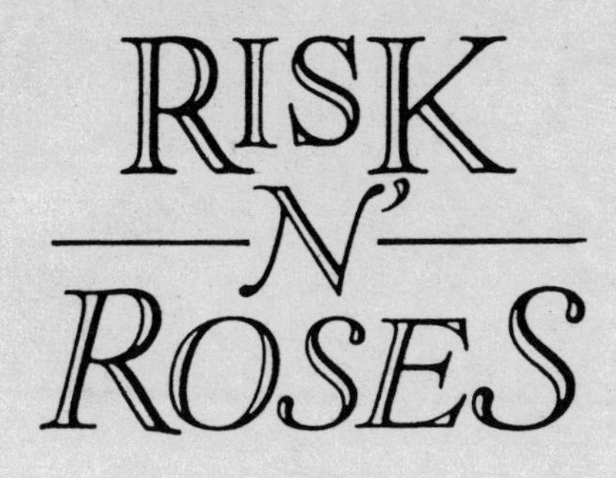
RISK
N'
ROSES

ONE

"Hurry," calls the street. "I'm waiting. After supper is the best time. It is high summer and we have hours to be together before Home calls you in from the dark. Come. Your life is out here with me. Your friends are here. The gang. You can forget everything but them in the slap of your running feet. I give you fun and freedom and risk. Oh yes, risk. Sometimes I can be dangerous. Daring is also my name, and I can tempt you to put your hand into the lion's mouth."

"Can I be excused?" said Skip. She pushed her chair away from the supper table, ready to run. Noise from the street filtered through the open windows like news of the world. It made her feet itch to get outside.

Her mother held the glass for Angela. Milk dribbled from Angela's chin to Mrs. Berman's hand, cupped underneath to catch the drops.

"Toss me that dishtowel, will you? We just ironed this blouse this afternoon, didn't we, sweetie?"

This last was said to Angela, who moaned deep in

her throat and reached for the glass. She twisted it away from her mother and spilled what was left of the milk on her lap.

Skip handed her mother the towel. "She can hold it by herself, Mom. She does with me. Can I go now?"

Angela patted her wet skirt, smiling at the sticky sounds it made. The next instant she held her skirt away from her body and looked apologetically at her mother.

Mrs. Berman pursed her lips and considered Skip's request. "You are just going to sit outside on the steps?"

"I guess."

"Don't guess. Stay there. I'll get her changed and you can take her with you."

The protest sprang out of Skip's mouth. "Aw Mom, no!" Not yet. Not tonight with Angela around her neck. What if one of the kids on the block came over? What if that girl did?

For the past five days, ever since they moved to this busy street, Skip had sat on her front steps watching and sorting out what went on out there like a fan at a baseball game.

There was one girl she liked already. She lived across the street next to the house with the roses, and looked to be about eleven, Skip's age. Whenever this girl came out of her house, Skip saw how the other kids left what they were doing and ran over to her. Everyone wanted to play with her. Suppose that girl came over and started to talk. And Angela was there . . .

"Wait right here," said Mrs. Berman, as if she

hadn't heard Skip. She stood and pulled Angela up with her.

At fifteen, Angela was as tall as her mother. She was a pale-haired rounded beauty in contrast to her younger sister, who was still all bones and elbows. Rose White and Rose Red her father used to call them, after the fairy tale of the two sisters, one so pale and blond and the other dark-haired and red-cheeked. "Where are my Roses?" he'd call out as soon as he came home from work.

He had stopped calling them that when the differences between them became clearer.

While Skip waited for Angela she wandered into the living room. The Oriental rug hadn't come from the cleaners yet and her footsteps on the bare floorboards made the room sound emptier than it was. The furniture from the other apartment was there: the green couch that opened up, the glass-topped coffee table, her father's black leather chair with the hassock in front of it. She liked to sit on the hassock and lean against his legs while he listened to Lowell Thomas on the radio. The big Zenith was against a different wall now. All the furniture was familiar, but the room wasn't. It didn't feel like home yet.

She went to look out of the big bay window that fronted the street. The curtains weren't up so she had a clear view. The street outside seemed more like home than any room in the house.

It was half past six on a muggy August evening in 1948. The sun was still high. It glittered off the windows of the row of houses across the street. They were separated from one another by alleys just wide enough for a car to drive through to the garage in back.

What Skip marveled at was how different the houses were from one another. She had come from a street of tall buildings, every one the same and all tan like dirty sand. Here, big wooden houses with wide porches were next to small brick ones like the one she was in now. They were all sizes and shapes, some were fancy and some were run down. "A real hodgepodge," she heard her mother say about the block.

For Skip, coming from a high-rise apartment house in New York City, this backwater street in the Bronx was new and strange and splendid. Where she used to live she was never allowed out after supper. "Too dangerous," said her father, meaning the elevator down and all the heavy buses and trucks driving past. Here there was hardly any traffic. She could just step out of the house and there she was, like living in a playground.

From the window, Skip saw that the nightly game of hide-and-seek had started up the block near the grocery store. She could already recognize some of the kids. There were the fat red-headed twins making pests of themselves. They were holding hands at arm's length and running down the street forcing everybody to go around them. Some small girls had begun their evening jump-rope marathon and in the middle of the street, right in front of her window, the bigger boys were starting up their stickball game.

So much running around, so much play. The whole street seemed in motion, like lifting a log to uncover ants on the move.

Her attention was drawn to the house directly opposite, the one with all the flowers out front. Something was going on. Some kind of fight maybe. The man she knew only as Kaminsky was standing in his doorway. He was waving his arms at a girl facing him at the foot of his steps and he was angry.

Skip couldn't hear what he was saying, but she could see his mouth open and close. Like a puppet on a string, she thought to herself, giggling at the idea.

The girl had her back toward Skip so she couldn't see her face. She could tell from the defiant way she stood with her hands on her hips that she was angry too.

Something definitely was going on. Impatience tore at Skip as usual, making her feet move restlessly. She couldn't wait to get out there.

Her mother finally appeared and said, "All right, you two, out you go." Nothing pleased her more than to see her two girls together just like other sisters.

Angela now wore a crisp pinafore a few shades lighter than the cream of her skin, and better suited for someone younger. Her long fair hair was smooth, parted in the middle and held in back by a wide barrette. It framed her face which her mother claimed resembled the paintings of madonnas in museums. A cigar box that held her precious buttons was clasped to her bosom with one hand. The other hand she stretched out to her sister with a wet happy smile.

Three wide brick steps led from their doorway to the sidewalk. Skip sat Angela on the top step and she settled next to her to watch the show.

She heard the man, Kaminsky, say with a funny accent, "Now you listen to me, Jean Persico. I already told you too many times. Stay out of my garden. Play someplace else. You hear me? You got ears? I'm warning you. I'll fix you good. Stay away from my roses." He waved at them with the same hand that held a tennis ball.

Skip had seen him working in his garden. It was just a small plot with a low picket fence around it. It didn't take up much room but it was filled with roses. On a street where people used the small patch of ground out front to park the baby carriage or let the kids dig in, his was the prettiest place on the block.

She had seen his lips moving as he tended his flowers, as if he were talking to them. She hadn't paid much attention, being far more interested in what went on in the street than in a crazy old man who talked to himself.

Kaminsky's voice was deep and loud. Angela stopped sorting the buttons and looked up at the noise. It was the roses that caught her, not the fight. She stood up and cried, "Flowers!" stretching out a begging hand.

"Shhh!" ordered Skip, pulling her down again. Later she would take her sister across the street and let her touch the petals. She knew that was what she wanted.

The girl across the street was shouting back at Kaminsky. "Oh yeah? You're gonna fix me? You and who else? President Truman?"

Skip was thrilled. She couldn't imagine talking to a grownup that way. If she even raised her voice to her parents she was punished. Besides, now she could see that this was the same girl! This was the one she had been watching from these same steps for so many days, the one she already had a crush on.

Her lips shaped the air. "Jean Persico," she said to herself reverently. Now she knew her name.

Kaminsky had on only a sleeveless undershirt beneath the wide black suspenders that held up his stained garden pants. He was still a big man, but the skin of his upper arm was thin and the flesh from his chest and shoulders had slipped downwards, collecting in a soft heap at his middle. His hair was a circle of gray steel wool around a bald spot, and his broad flat face was creased with age. But his eyes were sharp and were now narrowed into slivers of blue ice.

He kept those eyes on Jean Persico for a few seconds and then turned, ready to go back inside his house. But the girl wasn't finished with him.

"Give me back my ball!" she yelled. "It's a free country. I can play where I want and you can't stop me. I'll get my brothers on you. Hitler! Hitler! Why don't you go back where you came from?"

Kaminsky turned back to her. His face had flushed an ugly red. He seemed to swell and fill the doorway.

Skip thought to herself, uh-oh, tensing up, expecting something bad to happen. He looked to her like a man ready to explode or throw something heavy. Instead, he breathed hard the way people do when they are trying to control themselves, and shook his head at the girl below. He tossed the ball to her.

"You're a no-goodnik," he said without heat. "Get away from here with your bad mouth. You don't know what you say. Play someplace else." He went into his house.

Jean Persico didn't give up. She yelled at the closed door. "Yellowbelly, shakes like jelly."

She threw the ball at his steps. It hit a rim and flew up and over her head to drop in the middle of the street. It bounced, seemingly out of the sky, in front of a boy running to the manhole cover which was third base. When it landed, he paused just long enough to get tagged out. Furious, he gave the tennis ball a kick and like a gift from heaven above, it sailed over to Skip, who jumped up and neatly caught it on the fly.

Laughing all the way, Jean ran over to her.

Skip handed her the ball. "Here," she said, also laughing, but she wouldn't have been able to say at what. It was partly the look on the boy's face when the ball dropped in front of him, partly the way he kicked it, like he wanted to kill it. And also how it landed right in her hand. Mainly she laughed because here she was, talking to Jean Persico.

"Nice catch," said Jean in a husky voice. She was swarthy and skinny, a little taller and a little older than Skip. Maybe closer to twelve. Her stringy brown hair needed washing. There was a space between her front teeth, and her nose had a bump in the middle. Her flowered play dress was too small for her and had a tear under the armpit. Inside it her body moved with the grace of a natural athlete. Skip thought she looked just the way everyone should.

Jean Persico bounced the ball a few times and then said, "You're new around here. I seen you. I thought you had a gimpy leg or something, just sitting all the time, watching me. You a spy or something?" She grinned at this, showing pink gums. "What's your name, anyhow?"

"Skip. Skip Berman."

This was real funny. "Hey, what kind of name is that? Skip the Drip. Skip the mustard. How come? It's a nickname, right?"

"Yeah. My real name is Amy Louise, but nobody calls me that. My daddy says I'm always in a rush even when I was a little kid. He says I learned to skip real early and that's what I did mostly. So that's what they started calling me and it stuck."

"Skip. Yeah. Okay. I like it. Mine's Jean."

"I know. I heard that man, you know, across the street just now. He called you that."

"Oh him," said Jean, wrinkling her nose as if she smelled something bad. "Everybody hates him. He thinks that dump of his is sacred like the church, we can't play there." She turned fierce. "Nobody yells at me. Nobody!" Again she changed. This time she was full of wicked laughter. "I fixed him. Know what I did to him the other night?"

"No, what!" It was sure to be something so bad and so fun that Skip was breathless with wanting to know.

Jean's impudent hazel eyes measured her. "I think I better not. I don't think I'll tell you yet. It's secret. Maybe you are a spy. How do I know?"

Skip laughed with her but she was inwardly gasping. She had had friends before. Always, always she needed to have friends. Her mother had complained more than once that they were too important to her. "Family comes first," she had said, meaning Angela.

Her mother got angry when she found out that Skip gave away things to her friends: her bears, her books, once her new sweater.

"Why do you do that?" her mother had wanted to know. Skip had no way of explaining that it eased something hungry in her, that all she wanted was to be loved back.

But they were ordinary, those friends. Like Skip, they were, not like Jean Persico. She had never met anyone like her before. Being with her was like stepping off the path in a strange wood. You weren't sure of where you were.

She even smelled different. Behind the sun-warmed skin and the day's run-around dirt was something else. Something sharp and delicious like a Fourth of July firecracker, the smell of dazzle and danger.

TWO

Skip was totally absorbed by her new friend. Her sister Angela was forgotten.

She heard someone calling Jean's name above the hubbub of the street.

"Be right there," shouted Jean.

Skip couldn't see who had called her, since a line of kids skated by just then, blocking her view. She hated whoever it was. Jean was being taken away just when they were making friends.

"That dumb Francine," said Jean, poking her head at the unseen caller across the street. "She doesn't let me be. I swear, she'd follow me into the bathroom if I let her. Can you imagine?"

Skip shook her head to show how hard it was for her to imagine such a ridiculous thing. At the same time she saw herself on her knees, following Jean anyplace, including the bathroom.

"Well, so long. When you gotta go, you gotta go." Jean took a few jaunty steps away, stopped, and looked back at Skip. "Hey, you want to do something with us?"

Reprieve! "Sure!" Skip didn't care what.

"Me and my friends are gonna break into an empty house. Norma says it's haunted but you can't believe a thing she says. She's afraid of her own shadow. So, come on then. It's in the next block."

Skip's feet rushed her to Jean's side before her head caught on to what she was doing. Angela. She suddenly remembered. She couldn't leave her and she couldn't take her with her.

Skip looked at her sister playing with her dopey buttons, not even knowing she was blocking her way. If Angela had a gun aimed at Skip to keep her from going with Jean Persico, it wouldn't stop her more effectively than just the sight of her sitting there, the simple fact of her.

A hot lump gathered in Skip's throat. The familiar feeling of "It's not fair!" swept through her once again, as it had so many times before.

Jean pulled her arm. "Come on, then." Her husky voice held a note of command which made it all the harder for Skip to tell her, "I can't."

"Hey, you just said . . ." Jean gave her a blank stare that said I don't know you anymore. "Okay with me. See you around." She tossed the ball up in the air, caught it, and was ready to move on.

Skip knew she was losing her. "No, wait! It's her. I can't go on account of my sister." She pointed to Angela, whose pure profile hid her slack mouth and child eyes. "I have to stay with her. I forgot."

"Oh yeah?" Jean was amused. "What is she, your baby-sitter? I'll fix it for you. She can come too if she wants."

Before Skip could stop her, Jean stepped up to Angela and said, "Your sister is coming with me. Want to come along?"

Angela looked up and smiled as she had been taught to do at nice people. Then behind Jean she saw her sister, whom she adored. As if she hadn't seen her in a year she spread her arms out to her. Joy made them unstable. "Skip, Skip, c-c-come look!" she cried, holding out a button. There was a hint of stutter, a soft slurring of the words. Her voice was high and clear and sweet.

She held out another button to Jean to be polite. "You can hold one if you w-want."

Jean Persico stared at her, sizing her up. She took a step backward and passed a finger under her nose. Without taking her eyes from Angela, or bothering to lower her voice, she said to Skip, "What's wrong with her?"

"She was born like that. You know, slow. She's going to a special school here. That's why we moved here." Skip's skin itched with embarrassment. This was what she had dreaded.

Angela listened to this as if hearing a favorite bedtime story. She nodded eagerly. "In my school they're gonna t-t-teach me things. I c-c-can get a job."

Jean found this funny. "What kind of job can you get?"

Angela puckered her forehead and looked at her sister with puzzled eyes. "What k-kind of job, Skip?"

Jean was studying Angela the way she would an odd plant or a food she hadn't seen before. Then she shrugged as if she had seen enough. Impatiently she said to Skip, "So what's the big deal? Can't she stay by herself? I had a dog once, I'd tell him to stay and he'd stay. Tell her and let's go." She yelled again across the street, "I'm coming, keep your shirt on."

The sun's rays still lingered on the rooftops, making a canopy of light over the noise and motion of the street. The hide-and-seek game was in full cry at one end of the block. The jump ropes, both single and double dutch, were played mostly in the middle of the street and at the other end was the stickball game. Weaving in and out of these sacred zones were children on roller skates or on homemade scooters, or bikes. Anything that rolled.

The street was alive and kicking, and Skip couldn't bear to be out of it anymore. Something rebellious took hold of her and shook her and couldn't be resisted. She could tell Angela to stay and she'd stay, the way Jean said. She'd be okay here alone for a while and nobody would ever know.

Never before had she left her sister when she was supposed to be in charge. It was as if contact with Jean Persico had already changed her, made her bolder, like catching the flu.

She said to Angela, "Mom says you have to mind me so you have to stay right here. Don't go away. I'm going someplace with Jean for a little while, okay?"

"Okay."

"Come on now, you have to promise. Say, 'I promise I won't go away.'"

Skip wanted her to say it, so she did.

Jean grabbed Skip's hand and ran across the street

with her, dodging the runners, paying no attention to the kids who called out Hi to her as she sped by.

They ran to the two girls who were sitting on the curb playing jacks. Skip had seen them with Jean the past few long ago days when she was just a watcher.

The chubby girl with the long finger curls hanging down her back said in a whining way, "Where were you? Norma was scared. She thought Kaminsky got you, right, Norm?" She nudged the smaller girl sitting next to her, who looked up at Jean with big dark eyes and nodded in agreement. "I was scared," she echoed. Norma had a high whispery voice that suited her heart-shaped face.

"You're always scared," said Jean, grinning, showing the gap between her teeth that Skip already envied. Skip saw that Jean liked this Norma being scared like a baby. Norma lifted her straight black bangs from her eyes and smiled up at them as if she had been handed a compliment.

Pudgy Francine watched this exchange and to get Jean's attention said loudly, "Hey, you got the ball! I knew you'd get it back!" Admiration was all over her heavy face.

Jean said, "Kaminsky said he saw you throw the ball, and I should tell you to watch out or else next time it's the police."

Francine scrambled to her feet and looked wide-eyed at Kaminsky's garden a few houses down the street from where they were. She couldn't get the words out fast enough. "I did not! Did he really say that? You threw it, remember? Come on, not me, honest! Did he say . . . he said I was. . . ?" She was floundering.

Jean relented and told her she was just kidding. "Boy, you'd swallow anything. I really had you going." She laughed, digging a finger into Francine's side until she got her laughing, too.

Then a careless arm was draped over Skip's shoulder as Jean introduced her. The nickname had to be explained in full. "She's coming with us to the house." With a flick of her teasing eyes at Francine, she added, "She's my best friend."

Skip swallowed spit and tried to stop the silly grin she felt rising to her lips. The words "best friend" were knocking around in her rib cage. She felt Francine's jealous eyes on her.

Little Norma said "Hi," with a friendly smile. She said to Jean, "We have to wait for Ellie. I wonder what story she's telling her mother this time."

Jean said, "Who cares? We won't wait anymore. She gives me a pain always blowing her nose all the time."

"Me too," said Francine.

The sun had set, but it was still light out, still too early for the street lamps. Jean sent Francine for a flashlight in case it was dark inside the house they were about to explore.

Before they set out, Skip quickly glanced at her own house across the street, making sure that Angela was still sitting where she had left her. Then she blinked hard in an effort to forget her.

Jean led them up the street, holding the flashlight above her head, swinging it, lifting her legs high as if leading a parade. "Follow the leader," she ordered.

The other girls copied her, marching behind, full of giggles at the game. Skip watched her every move closely, wanting to do as she did, wanting to be her.

They passed Abchek's grocery store, which stayed open late in the summer. Jean picked up an orange from the stand outside as she marched past. But before the other girls could "follow the leader," she was caught. Mr. Abchek flapped his apron at her and yelled for her to return it or pay.

She tossed it back onto the stand with a scornful laugh and dashed across the street, followed closely by the three other girls. In the middle of the next block she halted in front of a house with a single board nailed across the front door. The house was so run-down it looked drunk. The roof sagged and some shingles were hanging loose. No curtains on any window, except for one on the right side on the second floor. That one had a rag of a curtain halfway down. Skip thought it made the window look like a horrible eye winking at her. The house loomed above them dark and unwelcoming, and made them want to whisper.

Norma said, "It's haunted. I told you it was." She laughed in a high pitched nervous way.

"What'll we do now, Jeanie?" asked Francine. "It's all boarded up."

Jean was studying the house, looking it over, tapping the flashlight on her palm. "Wait here a minute," she said, and went around to the back.

Without her presence, assurance leaked out of the girls like air out of a balloon.

Skip couldn't help thinking of Angela. A screen of pictures unrolled behind her eyes that showed her mother screaming, Angela under a car, her father's outraged eyes, and herself in rags, banished from her family, begging for food. All this she saw in her mind's eye before Francine had finished saying, "It sure looks spooky."

"What if we're caught?" Norma looked up and down the quiet street as if she expected the police any moment. This block, so close to their own, was different. Here the houses were larger, more grand, with trees and lawns.

"Where's everybody?" Francine whispered. It was as if the street had been tipped so that all the natural noise and jumping life had slid to their end.

With Jean gone Skip's conscience awoke and stung her like an angry bee, making her take a few steps toward home. She could tell these girls she had to go to the bathroom.

Jean appeared from around the side. It was too late for flight. The sight of Jean waving her arm, signaling them to come with her made Skip's conscience go to sleep again.

"There's a broken window out back," Jean told them with a triumphant grin. "We can climb in easy. Nothing to it."

Skip ran to her along with the others, hoping that nothing about her would give away the shameful fact that breaking into an abandoned house was as far from her ordinary life as a walk on the moon.

THREE

Open bags of garbage spilled out on the small yard at the rear of the house. It had a chain fence around it but it was obviously used as a dump. The girls had to step carefully over broken bottles and rotting food.

"Phew, what a stink!" said Francine.

Norma was holding her breath. A hand covered her open mouth as if to stop all those germs from entering, or perhaps to keep her supper from exiting.

"Look there," said Jean, pointing. "See what I mean?"

Above their heads, one of the first-floor windows was broken. Some jagged pieces of glass remained in place, making it dangerous to climb through.

Skip said to herself, "What next?" the way she did when she read storybooks. She felt she was in one now.

"Get that box over there," ordered Jean to no one in particular.

Francine went for it but Skip was quicker. She didn't notice the look of jealousy Francine gave her as she dragged the wooden crate over to Jean. Standing on the box, Jean smashed out the remaining glass with a stick. Now they could safely enter.

Inside, they found themselves in a large vacant room made darker by the grime on the walls and blackened floorboards. They decided it was once the living room because of the tipsy chandelier dangling overhead and the boarded up fireplace. They continued through the rooms on the first floor without speaking, Jean pointing with the beam of her flashlight to the cracks and chunks of broken plaster in the ceiling and walls. The evening light still poured in through the blank windows, but she had switched on the flashlight.

The girls came to a room with empty shelves from floor to ceiling. Skip knew they were for books. So the people who had lived here liked to read. What else could she tell about them by looking around? Why they had left? The room had a funny smell: musty, old . . . bad. Maybe the house was really haunted and the owners had been scared away.

She was scaring herself by thinking this when Jean said, "Tramps," shining the flashlight on a pile of bunched-up newspapers in a corner. It could have been used as a bed. There were some empty beer bottles nearby and cigarette butts on the floor.

"Maybe they're still here!" cried Norma, who moved closer to the reassuring beam of light. Francine was already at Jean's side.

Skip noticed a bobby pin on the floor and picked it up to show to them. "Not tramps," she said. "Look at this. It comes from a girl!" She was a detective on a case, able to read clues as easily as reading words in a book. "Lovers," she told them in a hushed voice.

"Running away from their families who were sworn enemies. They weren't allowed to meet and so they had to come here." It all seemed somehow familiar as she said it. "They came here to die. A suicide pact. Maybe they're upstairs." She was inspired.

Francine giggled. Norma inhaled "aaaah" on a breath. Jean beamed the flashlight on Skip's face and held it there for an instant. "Yeah," she said, making her husky voice even deeper. "They're dead upstairs. Let's find the bodies."

An exquisite shiver shot through Skip. Jean had turned Skip's made-up story into the real thing.

Jean led them to the wide steps that went upstairs to the second floor. They stood at the bottom and looked up. Above them was a cave of darkness.

"They're up there," intoned Jean, holding the flashlight under her chin and bulging her eyes. Norma yipped like a scared rabbit.

Jean began to climb without a trace of fear.

Usually Skip bounded up steps. This time her feet were stuck in molasses. She kept a hand on the banister and her eyes on the circle of light ahead. The other hand was clasped in Norma's. In front of them climbed Francine, holding on to the back of Jean's dress. No one spoke. Only the creak of the stairs could be heard as they slowly moved up.

When they reached the landing, they huddled together like cows in the rain as Jean played the light around to see what was there. There were four doors in a row, all of them closed, all of them needing to be opened, "But please God, not by me," prayed Skip.

It was Francine who whispered urgently, "Let's go!"

Skip and Norma nodded without knowing it.

"You scared?" Jean asked Francine. Her voice was normal, as if they were out in the street at midday. "Go ahead home. Nobody's stopping you. Go on, why don't you." Her scorn could flay skin. Skip drew in an awed breath.

"Don't be like that." Francine whined this like someone whipped. "It's getting late and my mother'll kill me."

Skip felt the knife slide right through her belly. Killing was minor compared to what was going to happen to her. Angela! Her sister's image dangled in front of her like a bad dream.

Always, always all her life she had to be the good girl, had to make it up to Them because of her sister. If her parents knew that she had left Angela to break into somebody's house they wouldn't think she was the good girl now. She could imagine her father's surprise and displeasure if he knew what she was doing, and here she was, doing it anyway.

She concentrated on watching Jean test the door knobs. Two of them were locked. The next knob turned easily.

Jean whispered in a grim voice, "The dead bodies must be in here."

Skip was sure the other girls could hear her heart thumping.

Jean pushed the door open. The three girls behind her shrieked and hid their faces so as not to see the horror inside. She poked her head inside and laughed aloud.

"Hey, what a place! Come see!" she said.

They all crowded in the doorway.

The blessed light of the late afternoon was filtering through two filthy windows on the far wall. It showed them a plain ordinary room like any other. Perhaps once a bedroom.

Wallpaper of faded cabbage roses and green leaves looped around the walls or hung down in strips. There was a shallow closet with its door hanging off the top hinge. A few wire clothes hangers still clung to the bar in a lopsided row. The window panes were unbroken. One of the windows still had a rose-print curtain hanging forlornly from a single hook. The room was in good shape. There were no bodies, dead or otherwise.

Francine and Norma poked around the room noisy with relief, telling one another how scared they had been over nothing.

Skip leaned against the wall near the door. She was still a bit shaky in the legs, her imagination having floated to her mind bloated bodies, eyeless sockets, lolling tongues. She watched Jean Persico prance around the room and was certain that her new friend was the bravest person that ever was.

In the far corner near one of the windows was a blue velvet armchair spilling its stuffing onto the wooden floor. Jean ran to the chair and plopped herself on it, raising puffs of dust.

The room was sticky hot, full of the closed-up musty smell typical of the house. Skip managed to open one of the windows to let in some air. It wasn't much cooler than the inside but at least it was fresher.

She leaned on the sill to look down at the backyard. There was the box they had stood on to climb in. She looked up and the sky was streaked with dark. The moon was rising. Across the way were the backs of houses with lighted rooms behind drawn shades. Over the rooftops rose the glow of street lamps signaling the end of outside play and the beginning of night.

What time was it? She had to get home! And yet, when she turned to say so, she couldn't. She didn't want to leave yet. Something was being forged in that room, she felt it. Norma was curled like a kitten on the arm of Jean's chair. Francine leaned on crossed arms over the back of it. At the center, lit up like the moon, sat Jean smiling at her. Skip, in love, grinned back. The others were Jean's friends and so they would be hers too. She felt as if she had known them all for ages instead of for one single astonishing evening.

The light was draining from the room. In that moment of quiet Jean Persico left her chair in a swift movement. She tore the faded print curtain from its hook to drape it from her shoulders. Pretending to be a queen she strutted around the room, the curtain dragging behind like the train of a majestic gown. She stepped out with her chin in the air as if she owned the air she moved through.

Norma and Francine fell into step behind her. Skip curtseyed as the queenly curtain went by, laughing with the others at this make-believe. But underneath everyone knew that there was a seriousness to the game.

Jean stopped her regal walk. Her lively face went blank in thought. Finally she nodded to herself, satisfied. "That's it!" she cried, spreading her arms as if she had made a great discovery.

She had an announcement to make. They were told that from now on this room belonged to them. They had found it, didn't they? Finders keepers.

She said to them, "It's our secret room. This is where we can hold our meetings." She told them that if anyone was too chicken to come there for meetings they had to say so. They had to swear to God on their mother's life that they wouldn't tell about this room. If they told anyone they would be a traitor and everyone knows what happens to traitors.

Her rapt audience looked at one another and then back to her.

Skip was thrilled to the core. Secret meetings. How she was going to manage she didn't know except that somehow she would. If it meant dropping Angela down a manhole into the sewer, she would.

Francine was the first to speak up. "Sure. It's a great idea. I swear, they could torture me and pull out my fingernails, I wouldn't tell."

Norma said, "Okay Jean, but what are we going to meet here for?"

Jean took Norma's question seriously. "You're right. There has to be a reason. I don't know it yet but I'll think of it and it will be something so terrific that . . ." She shaped something high and wide with her hands. Words failed her.

She glanced at the window and saw the deepening dark. "What time is it?" she cried. "I gotta get home!" She frantically tore off her queen's robe and threw it on the floor. Without another word she ran for the door.

"The flashlight!" wailed Norma. They all dashed after her in order to see their way out of there.

What shot through Skip's mind as she ran was that Jean Persico, who was the bravest person in the whole world, was also scared of going home, just like anybody else. Just like her.

FOUR

Now there was an empty space next to Angela where before there was usually somebody—her sister, her mother, a teacher, always somebody. The emptiness felt strange to her. She swayed, moving her body around, testing the sudden feeling of looseness.

She wanted to move some more. Her legs said move. She pushed away her box of buttons and stood up.

Across the street were Kaminsky's flowers and they shouted to Angela. Once again she stretched out her hands to them and this time Skip wasn't there to say shhh, sit down. Everything else on the street seemed to go by too fast or else was too still. The children at their games were a blur of movement and the other houses on the block had nothing to hold her eyes. But Kaminsky's flowers were an explosion of color that she wanted to touch. Her fingertips could already feel the soft petals.

Angela had a collection of velvet material that she kept under her pillow. They were pieces of color that pleased her eye and hand. At night she touched them one by one before she slept and named the color aloud in the darkness.

When she was little she once touched her new nightie and said, "Red. It feels red." Her mother still repeated that story. "She can actually feel color!" she would say, shaking her head at such cuteness. What her eyes said was, See how extraordinary my daughter is? In certain ways.

Red was Angela's favorite color although her mother always dressed her in white. Mrs. Berman said it suited her and didn't mind all the washing and ironing. She said it was her pride and her joy to keep her daughter looking so nice, so beautiful. Angela had heard her mother say that to her father and he had yelled that it was also her penance. Once she had asked Skip what penance meant and was surprised that Skip didn't know. Skip knew everything.

Angela kept her eyes on the flowers across the street and went to them. Down one step, another step and then another. She reached the sidewalk and kept on going. She had forgotten that Skip had said to stay. She forgot that she was not allowed to cross the street. She forgot everything but what she was after.

She reached the curb, stepped down and started across, walking in a slow, toes-in way that made her sway a bit from side to side. She walked as if her shoes hurt. Her eyes were for the garden and on her lovely face was a wide happy smile.

She paid no attention to the children who miraculously dodged her as they ran past. Halfway across the street she plowed right through the stickball game still in full swing.

"Hey, watch where ya going, cantcha?"
"Wattaya, blind?"
"C'mon, hurry up!"

She kept on going in her deliberate way, her eyes on the flowers, zoomed in like a camera on what she was after.

She stepped up on the curb. A few steps more and she was at Kaminsky's low fence, at the flowers behind it. Roses. They were roses. She knew what they were called.

For a long moment she did nothing but stare. Up close they were all so different from one another. Some were just budding, some were in full flower. There were snowy white ones, some yellow like butter, reds, purples. Some were striped like candy canes at Christmas.

She had to get closer. Angela found the side gate and at last she was where she wanted to be, in the middle of the garden. There she turned around and around with her arms outstretched like a lover. She was bowled over. The roses were such a surprise to her.

She had seen flowers before. Her mother had let her go into stores that sell them, and sometimes her father brought some home. She was allowed to put them in water. Also one of her jobs was to water her mother's plants.

But never had she been so close to so many roses at once. The thorns didn't stop her. Her fingers exulted in the soft petals, handling them carefully so they wouldn't mind. She bent to put her nose to a red one, to a pink one, to the purple one here and the golden one there. She was in smell heaven.

Angela didn't notice or care that as she moved around, her dress snagged and her legs were scratched from the thorns. She bent to sniff a flower, reached out to touch another, going about the roses like some absorbed and drunken bee. She wasn't aware of the sounds from her throat, the ones that came when she was taken by happiness.

Suddenly there was a roar at her ears. Someone grabbed her arm. "What do you think you're doing!" She saw a red swollen face and icy eyes close to her own. Her arm hurt. A shouting angry voice filled her ears.

She howled with fright.

Kaminsky stopped in confusion. He let go of her arm and made stop signs with his hands but the girl still wailed. Her eyes were staring wide and she shrank from him like a terrified child.

"Shah, shah," he said. He was able to lead her to his steps where he sat her down, meanwhile fishing out his handkerchief to mop her face.

"Okay, okay, okay. A big girl like you. Stop the noise already."

He kept his booming voice down and his movements slow in the way he used to quiet skittish farm animals.

He studied the pretty, tearful face, trying to puzzle out what he had here. "So, young lady, maybe you can tell me. What were you doing in my garden?"

She raised her clear blue eyes to him, eyes like clear blue glass, without depth or guile. He didn't scare her anymore.

"Pretty flowers," she said. "I l-like to touch flowers." She held up her hand and rubbed her thumb along her fingertips to show him.

She looked over at the patch of garden so close to where they sat. A slight breeze stirred the roses, sending out a hint of the fragrance abiding at the heart. "They smell good," she informed him and smiled with the pleasure of it.

He smiled back and nodded in agreement. Aloud and to the air he said, "So that's how it is. May God forgive me. I yelled at her."

Angela agreed with him. "You yelled." She didn't do anything. Why did he yell?

"Yes. Well. I'm real sorry about that. You want to see my roses? So next time ask me. I don't let nobody in my garden. You ask me, I'll let you. First you got to know how to treat them. You got a name?"

"Angela Dorothea Berman. I can write it f-f-for you."

"Much obliged. You are new here to this neighborhood. I see you sitting across the way with the other, the little dark one. Your sister, maybe?"

He lifted his big head to look across the street and Angela followed his gaze. The ballgame was over. A line of boys sat on the curb opposite. Past them she recognized her house. She hadn't seen it from this angle before. Square red brick with one, two, three steps. And there was her button box. Home.

"Skip. My little sister Skip. She w-went away with another girl . . . You yelled at the other g-girl too. I heard you."

Now he frowned. "I know who you mean. Jean Persico. She got off lucky I just yelled. I came this close to losing my temper." He showed her with his fingers how close. "A narrow escape she had. She's a no-good friend for your sister. Bad news is what she is. She bothers you, you come to Kaminsky. Yes?"

Angela said yes and looked puzzled. Bad news was what you read in the newspaper.

He introduced himself. "Teofil Kaminsky at your service." He lifted her hand and kissed it like a prince. It made her pull it away fast, giggling. "You can call me plain Kaminsky. Forty-five years in this country, and nobody says my first name."

"Kaminsky."

He slapped his knees and stood up. "Now that we have been introduced, come, I'll show you my roses. But you must be careful, you understand me? Something is ahead for them, hoo-hoo, something good." His thick dark eyebrows lifted. Mirth made his belly shake.

Then he noticed that Angela was rubbing her legs. Her hands had some blood on them and her legs were smeared with it. He realized this was the work of his thorns where they had pricked her.

He clicked his tongue, tsk-tsk, and held out his hand to help her up. "Later for the flowers," he said. "Right now we get you cleaned up. Come inside a minute, come."

His front door opened to a small hallway and on the right was the kitchen. So much white made Angela blink. A pattern of blue and white linoleum covered the floor, and there was a blue and white tablecloth on the round table under the window. Otherwise everything else, refrigerator, stove, walls, chairs, all were stark white, including the café curtains on the double window that looked out on the street.

What relieved the whiteness was a row of flower photographs behind glass on the far wall. They cast a glow of brightness and warmth and made Angela head for them at once.

Kaminsky stopped her. He took her to the sink to run water over her hands to get the blood off. As he dried them for her he said, "Sit. We'll have plenty of time for pictures after I fix you up from those thorns."

"Thorns hurt." Angela regarded her streaked legs reproachfully.

He sat her down at the little round table and went to get a clean dishcloth from the cupboard next to the refrigerator.

Angela meanwhile examined the straw placemat, and the salt and pepper shakers. She picked up the checked tablecloth to look under it. On top of the table near the window was a small ceramic squirrel sitting on a pile of paper napkins. She held it to feel its cool smoothness. She rubbed her lips over its cold glossy head.

Kaminsky noticed her pleasure. "You like my squirrel? My wife bought that in Atlantic City, oh, years ago."

Angela looked around the kitchen. "No wife."

"No wife," he said as he ran cold water over the cloth. He looked up at the ceiling and said again, this time with bitterness, "No wife." "Sophia" cried his guts and heart. He glanced quickly at the girl. Fortunately she was only interested in the squirrel.

He squatted before her and wiped the blood from

her legs with the wet cloth. He examined the scratches. "Not too bad. Wait here a minute, okay? I'll get something to put on them."

While he was out of the room Angela went right away to the pictures on the wall. They were large photographs of different roses, seven of them in a row. She had just seen them in Kaminsky's garden. She knew them!

Kaminsky stood behind her. "So. You look at my family. You want to be introduced?"

"Flowers! Not family!"

"Sure, flowers. My prize roses. But I'll let you in on a little secret, just between you and me. You like secrets?"

The smile she gave him stung his heart. It had been so long since anyone had smiled at him that way.

"I love secrets," she said with that uplift from getting a gift. "Can I t-tell Skip?"

Kaminsky clasped his hands behind him, and with his massive head thrown back studied the photos one by one as if he hadn't seen them before.

He said, "Each one of these roses has a name. This yellow beauty is called the Peace rose. That's other people's name for it. But to me, this is my Uncle Josef. A fine rose, Uncle Josef."

He walked to the next. "This gorgeous red is known as crimson glory. What do they know. Listen for its real name." With deep respect he said, "It's my Aunt Julka, may she live in Paradise."

One by one he named the roses. "My best friend and cousin Lech . . . my baby cousin Anna . . . Here is Aunt Cherka the drunk. I water her plenty."

He came to the last photograph and fell silent. Angela waited for him to tell her its name, but he said nothing. For a long moment he stood silent before it, studying it with hooded eyes. It was a luminous rose caught by the camera at a moment of perfection. The color was a blush, the pink of a baby's yawn. A pearly drop of dew remained on one of the petals.

Kaminsky turned away from this photograph and said to Angela, "So this is my family I got here on my wall." He raised and dropped his arms in a hopelessly sad gesture.

Angela had been following Kaminsky with her lips moving as he named each photograph. She was silently repeating the names to herself.

"What's this one's n-name?" she asked, pointing to the last pink rose. "You forgot."

"Forget? I should live so long. What it is, child, is not forgetting, but remembering too much. For this one I don't have courage. The name is waiting but I cannot. Not yet."

He shook his big head and said, "Enough already." He tapped one of the other photographs and said, "This beauty is going to do it for me. I got some of these Uncle Josefs blooming in my garden this minute. Best ever. It'll knock their eyes out, those judges. Come, sit down. I'll put this iodine on the scratches. Then we'll go outside and I'll show you my people."

It was then that Angela heard the yelling. She heard her name shouted over and over. "Angela! Angela!" Through the window she saw her mother running up and down across the street yelling her name.

Kaminsky heard it too and ran to the door. He yanked it open and shouted, "Missus! Missus! Over here!"

Her mother heard him. She saw the big man wave to her and then her Angela came out of this strange man's house.

FIVE

Angela's mother dashed across the street to her daughter. Her hair had slipped its knot and hung in clumps at the sides of her pale face. Her eyes were wild. She clutched Angela close, thrust her away to look her over and then clasped her to her bosom again.

Angela had come down the few steps of the house to meet her mother in the pathway. Kaminsky remained in his doorway.

Mrs. Berman cried out to him, "What were you doing with this child!"

Kaminsky dropped his how-do-you-do smile and drew himself up from his easy slouch. "Hey, Missus, hold your horses! I was cleaning her up. See there?" Her scratched legs had stopped bleeding. There was nothing much to see.

Mrs. Berman turned Angela's face to her own. "Look at me, Angela. Are you all right?"

"Sure Mama. S-see the flowers?"

"This man didn't do anything to you? I said look at me Angela."

Angela looked and her mother nodded. She knew

her daughter well enough to read all the signs. She was okay.

"You gave me such a fright! Where's your sister? Where is Skip?" She had hold of Angela's arm and was walking her toward the curb. The lush garden she was passing didn't exist for her.

Angela balked. She stopped walking and looked over her shoulder at Kaminsky who filled his doorway, watching them depart. "I w-w-want to stay, Mama. I want to see Uncle Josef."

This was too much. Mrs. Berman cried out in dismay, "There was someone else?"

Kaminsky heard this. He said to her, "No, no one else," and to the sky above he added, "I should only be so lucky."

"Angela never lies! She is incapable. She mentioned an uncle, another man."

Kaminsky had nothing more to say to such a person who thought such things about him. He had had a bellyful of injustice in his lifetime and didn't have to put up with this small potatoes. "Uncle Josef. Think what you want, Missus. I got nothing more to say."

Hotly she said to him, "Don't take that tone with me! You can't know what I think, or what I go through. My husband will have plenty to say even if you do not. Come, Angela."

"No, no, Mama, no!" Something was being taken from her that she wanted. "Kaminsky," she cried, holding out her arms to him or to the flowers, it wasn't clear which.

Kaminsky stared after them for a moment before going back inside, scratching his chest and shaking his head. That's what you get, he told himself. That's what you get for letting someone in.

When they reached their own house, Mrs. Berman sank on the steps with Angela to recover from what she had been through. She thrust the cigar box of buttons into her daughter's hands to stop her crying. She had the girl blow her nose into a handkerchief and smoothed her hair with a shaking hand.

It relieved her to give Angela a good talking to. "You must never, ever, go into a strange man's house or anywhere else alone." This was repeated several times so that it would sink in.

Her mother's voice sounded to Angela like a faraway drone, like a passing plane in the sky. She was accustomed to hearing it go on and on over her head without her having to listen. The sound of it was as comforting as her old blanket.

Mrs. Berman went on to complain about her younger daughter and how she didn't know what came over Skip to leave her sister like that. "Where is that girl! Look, the streetlights just came on and she isn't home yet. Don't I have enough to worry about? Where is she?" She stood to peer up the block for her and saw her husband walking toward them, a big rumpled man with a heavy step.

Soon Angela felt a dry kiss on her cheek. The black stubble of his beard scratched her face.

Max Berman listened patiently, one foot up on the bottom step as his wife told him of her fright. His tie was hanging loose, his shirt sleeves rolled up and his jacket was slung over his shoulder. A stained straw hat sat on the back of his head exposing thick dark hair that stuck in clumps to his forehead. His big good-natured face was indoor pale and sweaty from his muggy walk from the bus stop. As his wife spoke, his sad brown eyes never left his elder daughter as she counted out her buttons. "One for Daddy, one for Mama, one for Skip, one for Kaminsky."

"I want you to go over to him this minute, Max. There was someone else there too. Another man. Be firm for once. The nerve of him taking the child inside his house, no matter what. You go talk to Mr. Kaminsky."

"Kaminsky, Mama. No mister."

Max Berman sighed from his toes. "Not now, Ruth. I'm hot and tired and I've had a lousy day. Tomorrow night I'll talk to him. I'll tend to it. I don't like it either, her in someone's house. But you tell me Angela is okay and I can see that for myself. What I want to know is where is my Skip at this hour? It's not like her to leave the girl and run off."

He began a slow climb to the door, dragging every step. He was about to enter the house when Skip raced up.

"I can explain!" she panted. In her mind was a hazy concoction of a command visit to someone's sick grandmother who had no clocks in the house. She hadn't worked it out but inspiration would come. She certainly couldn't tell about breaking into a house and having a secret room there.

Her father held up his hand like a crossing guard. "Are you all right?"

"Yeah, sure Daddy. See, it was like this . . ."

Again he stopped her. "You left your sister alone?"

"Well, I had to, see, it was just for a little while and I thought . . ."

"I don't want to hear it. Inside, young lady."

Later that night he came into her room and sat on her bed while she was still hiccuping from her mother's furious scolding.

"Skip, I'm surprised at you. I thought you knew better. Your mother has enough to contend with, you know that. I depend on you not to add to her worries, and look what you did tonight." He paused and the silence was bad too. Her father said to her, "I'm disappointed in you. I want you to know that."

This was worse than her mother's yelling and telling her that she couldn't leave the house for the next three days.

Skip couldn't see his face, but his voice was faraway cold and she missed his big warm hand on her face. He usually smoothed her cheek as he kissed her goodnight. Tonight, everywhere in the room, all she felt and all she breathed was his disapproval.

He got up to go and she couldn't bear it.

"I'm sorry, Daddy."

The bedsprings creaked as he sat down again. In the dark he sounded loving again but sad. "All my hopes are on you, you know that. You're my consolation, my good girl. Who else do I have? You be a help to your mother, hear me?"

His expectations lay heavily on her. When the door closed behind him she kicked off her sheet. Even her short nightie was too much.

Eventually Skip fell asleep remembering how it was in that abandoned house with Jean. It was daring to break in, daring to poke around when it was scary. For that little while she had felt like a desperado, a sweet heady feeling entirely new to her. She smiled, her nose stuffed with crying. She slept.

The next morning the doorbell rang while Skip was having her second breakfast. Knowing that her father was displeased with her left her with a hole inside that felt very much like hunger. Whenever she thought of him she had to go to the kitchen and make herself another peanut butter sandwich.

She was doing this very thing when she heard Jean Persico's distinctive voice at the door. Nobody else could sound like velvet and sandpaper at the same time.

She could only hear her mother's side of the conversation.

"No, Skip may not come out. Sorry . . . What? No, she can't come to the door. We are just getting settled here. She'll be helping me with that for the next few days . . . Yes, I'll tell her you were asking. What's your name again, dear?"

When the door closed it seemed to Skip that her mother shut it on all that mattered to her. Now Jean and the other girls would get together in the secret room and forget her. She was doomed to miss out on everything all because of Angela.

She heard her mother's footsteps come toward the kitchen. Skip ran quickly back to her own room. She was supposed to be getting it ready for painting.

Her bedroom was a small box off the hallway. It was always a bit dark in there since it didn't get the sun, but Skip treasured it. For the first time she had a room of her own. She even had a desk of her own that her father had bought second hand. A small Philco radio sat on it, passed down to her when the family bought the big Zenith. She did her homework to "The Lone Ranger" and "The Green Hornet." Skip pulled the desk to the middle of the room to clear the wall for painting.

Something rattled the glass of the half-opened window. There was only one window in her room. It was long and low, facing the paved alley that separated her house from its neighbor. The only thing she usually saw out the window was the brick wall of the next house. Now, directly beneath her, close enough to touch, was Jean Persico.

"Ha! I knew you had to be in there somewhere. I got the right window first thing. I'm a fortune teller!" Jean served up her gap-toothed smile.

"Shhhhh. My mother! Oh hey, I heard you at the door just now. Am I ever glad to see you!" Skip's spirits zoomed. Jean had wanted to see her and wouldn't take no for an answer.

"Yeah, well, come on out. We're all set to clean up the room. I came to get you."

Skip kneeled on the floor and leaned out across the sill. "Oh, I can't, I just can't. You heard what my mom said. I have to stay inside here for three whole days. It's for leaving my sister."

"So what? You can climb out. It's not so high. You can jump."

Jumping down was a cinch. She could just put one leg over the sill and then the other. For one time-stopped moment, Skip wavered. Jean made it sound so easy. Then she shook her head. She just couldn't, that's all she knew. Something in her wouldn't let her.

Jean shrugged unsurprised. "Okay, so we're going

to go ahead. I'm thinking we should be a club. You know? That room and all. What do you say?"

Skip felt like falling to her knees and babbling with gratitude, Oh, me too? You mean me too? "Sounds good," was what she said.

"Yeah. Wow, what's that?"

In leaning out the window Skip's locket, a gold heart, swung from her neck by a thin chain. Jean pointed to it.

"You mean this? My father gave it to me. I got it last year for a birthday present."

"Oh hey, can I see it?"

Skip lifted it from her neck and handed it down. "Look inside. It has my baby picture. Isn't it awful?"

Jean examined the locket closely. She held it up by the chain, swinging it, admiring the gleam. "Is it real gold?" she wanted to know.

"I guess."

Jean couldn't take her eyes from it. She was about to pass it back up to Skip when she drew her arm back. "It's real pretty. Can I have it?"

Skip would have given her the hair from her head if she had asked, but this was serious stuff. When he had given it to her, her father had made a big thing of it. "For my little girl's tenth birthday. The end of the single digits," he had said. "This is for growing up."

All this passed through her head as she saw how much Jean liked the locket. She wanted that liking for herself desperately enough to say, "Sure," adding hastily, "But not for keeps. Maybe I'll have to have it back sometime, okay? Only if I have to. Okay?"

Jean already had it around her neck. She tucked it

inside the neck of her play dress. "Yeah, sure, thanks a lot." The all-out smile she gave Skip eased the sore place left by her father's displeasure.

Jean said, "So I was telling you we have to have a name for the club and Ellie says . . ."

Skip was about to ask who Ellie was when Angela burst into the room. All morning she had gone about the house singing "Jingle Bells," her favorite tune, because Skip was there and so was her mother and nobody was mad anymore.

She was still singing it as Skip pulled her head back from the window. The very sight of her sister's clear-eyed happy face made her want to bite.

"What do you want?" she demanded. In a different voice she said to Jean, "Just a second. It's my sister."

"Who are you t-talking to?" Angela went to the window and stuck her head out. Nice and cool in the alley. No sun. She looked down and met Jean Persico's unblinking stare.

"Hi," said Angela, smiling joyfully. It was so funny to talk to someone outside when she was inside. She knew this girl and had something to tell her. "Kaminsky says you're bad news. That's a joke on him. B-bad news is in the newspaper."

Jean Persico scowled up at her. She kicked the brick on the side of the house. "Oh yeah? He said that?" She nodded her tousled head as if she had something all figured out. "Well, I got a better joke for him."

Her mood had changed. She was through talking. She held up a hand to Skip as a good-bye, and in her long-legged graceful way, ran out of the shaded alley, back to the sun-filled street.

"Oh, I know," Angela said, after Jean left. She held up a finger to her temple. "Mama wants you to help her with the curtains in the dining room."

Skip darted to her mother, not aware of her feet touching the floor. She was in. That was all that mattered. She would buy or beg her way, but she was in. In the club, in with a bunch of other girls, in Jean's good graces, in.

SIX

Kaminsky sat in his easy chair in the living room, listening to the weather report. It had been the worst summer in years, the announcer said. Kaminsky glared at the radio irritably. So that was news? He wasn't dead yet, he was mopping up sweat like anybody else, so that he knew already. What he wanted to hear was the forecast. Maybe there was a break coming in the long hot spell. Maybe it would pour down rain and cool off. Give his garden a treat. He wouldn't have to keep the hose going so much, watering, watering, keeping his family alive and well. Not that you could trust those weathermen. They knew from nothing, those young pishers. But it would be nice to hear the words. He could picture his roses with their scalloped heads in the air, drinking in the rain with pollen lips.

The picture pleased him. He leaned back in his chair and closed his eyes, the better to enjoy it. Soon the news would be on and he'd hear more about that ballplayer, Babe Ruth. Dead at such a young age, such a shame. All day long the news had been full of it. The radio announcer got further and further away and the tinny voice became the sound of rain in his head. He dozed.

The doorbell rang and he awoke to darkness with a start, choking off a snore. Who could be at the door this hour? And why should he always have this spurt of fear at that sound? He turned on the lamp by the side of his chair and checked his watch. It was already after nine. Again the doorbell sounded. Again someone playing tricks on an old man? No, a finger had been lifted, the buzzing had stopped.

Kaminsky heaved himself out of his chair, leaving the permanent dents his body had carved on it over the years. He headed for the front door. Maybe it was one of those insurance fellas. Pests all of them.

"Who's there?" he asked. He wouldn't open if it was one of them. A man can't have peace in his own home.

"Max Berman, from across the street."

Kaminsky fumbled with the latch. "Who?" he said, as he opened the door. He didn't know any Bermans.

A tall pouchy-eyed man in shirtsleeves said, "Mr. Kaminsky? Good evening. I'm Berman, your neighbor from across the street. You remember my daughter Angela? Say hello to Mr. Kaminsky, Angela."

Angela held on to her father's hand. Kaminsky remembered her all right, stepping around his garden yesterday, poor noodle. She was a nice girl no matter what she had upstairs. He fixed her up and look at the thanks he got. Never again. A crazy woman for a mother this one has, he thought.

Angela gaped at him with pleasure. She said to her father, "Not m-mister, Daddy. I told you. Kaminsky." She could show her father how. "Hello, Kaminsky."

"Well, well. Look who's here. What can I do for you, Berman?"

The man cleared his throat and looked at his daughter. That seemed to stiffen him. "Can I talk to you for a few minutes, Mr. Kaminsky? It's about my Angela here. We'll just clear up a little something. You see, my wife . . ." He let go of his daughter's hand. "Uh, Angela honey, you go on home now. You've seen Mr. Kaminsky like I promised, so say goodnight like a big girl. Go on now, go."

To Kaminsky he said, "She carried on so when she heard I was coming over here that I had to take her. Go on home, Angie. Your mother is waiting for you."

Angela's eyes filled and overflowed. "Goodnight, Kaminsky." There was a rise in her voice, the beginning of a tantrum. "I want to see Uncle Josef!"

Mr. Berman gazed at Kaminsky reproachfully. "Uncle Josef. Yes. My wife said that my daughter . . . Excuse me, I have to ask. Angela was in your house? You and some relative? Can you explain this to me?"

Kaminsky made a sound of disgust. He was ready to close the door in his face. Why should he listen to this dirt? But there was the girl, looking at him with those eyes. They were his Sophia's eyes. The same clear blue color, the same trust.

He said to her, "Go tell your father about Uncle Josef. You remember. Go tell him."

Angela said, "So p-pretty, Daddy. All yellow. He's my favorite. C-can I see him?"

Her father ran his hand over his face and gripped

his chin. His puzzled eyes were on his child, trying to make sense out of what she said.

Kaminsky was tempted to leave it at that, but he was sorry for the man. He said, "Tell me something. Did you bother maybe to ask her? A snapshot on the wall she's talking about. A rose. A rose with a funny name, that's all. Josef. So that settles that. Anything else? I took her in the house to fix her scratches, she was in my garden. You got a nice girl there, Berman. You got nothing to worry about from me. Good-night."

"Wait! Wait a minute, Kaminsky. This is ridiculous. You see . . . my wife, well, she gets overwrought. You understand how it is." He gestured with his head at the girl by his side. He pulled out a handkerchief and wiped his face.

Kaminsky nodded gravely. "I understand."

Mr. Berman said, "I won't bother you any further. Please accept my apologies. Angela, time for us to go home."

"Kaminsky, can I see them? Just one l-look?"

"Who, please? Who's them?"

"You know, the family. Daddy, you see, too."

"You have children, Kaminsky?"

"Me? Nah. I know what she means. Pictures on the wall she means. I mentioned already. Come in, come in, let the girl take a look. Nothing wrong with her memory, that one. A real knack she has for flowers."

As he held the door open for them, he glanced at his garden. He breathed in deeply. His roses were broadcasting their fragrance on the night air. The street lamps were lit at this hour, their amber glow casting a friendly light on the dirt and scattered trash beneath. The children were inside, their games over. Without their animal spirits the street seemed hushed and emptied of energy, like some exhausted beast. There were a few evening strollers out for relief after the heat of the day. An occasional cry, shrill and angry, cut the soft evening air.

Kaminsky followed his guests into his house. He reached for the kitchen light. Max Berman said to him, "A knack you say she has? You really think so?" Then the smile left him as he watched his daughter at the wall of photographs. He shrugged, a man resigned.

Angela pulled her father over to look at them with her. She showed him Uncle Josef and the red one whose name was um, was Aunt um . . . Julka. "Isn't that right, Kaminsky?" she asked, gleeful, rocking with pride.

As she pointed to each one, her finger smudged the glass that covered the photographs. Kaminsky didn't stop her. He listened to her repeat the names he had told her the way he listened to Mozart. "My b-baby cousin Anna, my best friend Lech . . . This is Uncle Josef, Daddy."

Her father followed her finger from one photo to the other, clicking his tongue in appreciation.

She came to the last one and said, "This one has no n-name yet. It's waiting. Wuh-when will you name it, Kaminsky? So, so pretty."

When I run out of hope, said Kaminsky to himself. Soon enough.

Angela's father saved him from her question. "Beautiful flowers, Kaminsky, beautiful." He paused. "Are you a retired man? A garden like yours must take a lot of time."

Kaminsky grunted. "I'm retired since the war. Three years now, no more tool factory. Too old. I was master machinist once. See these hands?" They were calloused, gnarled as trees. "Now they are only good for growing roses."

He waved a hand at the wall photos. "These here I had in the flower show at the Temple last year, they made honorable mention. This year . . . well, we'll see."

He pressed his lips in a secretive smile and closed his eyes for a moment, the better to see in his mind's eye the blue ribbon, the first prize. He would get that for his family. It was what he could do and then they would rest.

At that moment the doorbell rang.

"Let me! I'll go. Mama lets me."

Kaminsky followed the girl to the door. The peal was insistent. Someone had a finger on it and wouldn't let up.

Like the other night thought Kaminsky. Same thing. Noise in the night.

The old alarm shot through him. Childhood terror. It was at night they would come to his village. Lowlifes . . . hunting Jews the way pigs hunt truffles. Aunt Julka hiding him in the potato sack . . . the burning . . . screaming . . . At night violence comes through the door. He had learned that early in life.

Still the doorbell jangled. His aunt's screams turned into his Sophia's screams, the nightmare that had pursued him the past ten years. Again he was back in Wolska, his village on the other side of the world. Again night . . . now Nazi soldiers bursting in . . . after Jews, like the scum from his childhood . . .

his wife Sophia . . . her mouth forever open in a cave of terror. His ears fill with her wild cry. He sees Nazi hands drag her away. She calls his name.

Kaminsky rubbed the sweat from his face to release himself from this craziness. It was a scene he was forced to replay over and over again. And it was all his imagination. He had to invent what must have happened. He wasn't even there, may he be cursed for all eternity for leaving her behind.

"All right, all right, I'm coming!" he yelled.

Angela opened the door. "Hello," she said. She greeted the air. Nobody was there. Yet the doorbell still rang. Angela clapped her hands over her ears and whimpered.

The two men stepped outside. There was no one even close to the house. Yet the infernal buzzing continued.

"Look here!" said Mr. Berman, examining the doorbell. A pin had been wedged into the rim to keep it pressed down. He pulled it out and the bell stopped ringing.

Angela took her hands away from her ears and Kaminsky grunted with relief. It was as if a dentist's drill had stopped boring into his head.

"Can you beat that!" said Max Berman holding up the pin. He was shaking his head at the silly mischief of it when he noticed the other man's pallor and his heavy breathing.

Kaminsky looked at the cause of his distress. "Ach, I should have known. The same thing last week. Again a pin. Such a stupid thing. For what? For why?"

Angela's father was indignant on Kaminsky's behalf. "This happened before you say? What goes on here?" He looked about the neighborhood once again as if some clue were out there. The night was peaceful. There was nothing and no one to be seen to account for the pin.

Mr. Berman was at a loss. "A prank do you think? Some kid's idea of a joke?"

"Sure, a joke," said Kaminsky. He attempted a kind of smile. He wanted to keep to himself that once you were a victim of pointless cruelty, even a pin would seem a menace.

Above all he wanted to go inside and lock his door and be alone. He would be able to steady himself. Calm down. "They had their fun. I'll say goodnight now," he told the Bermans.

Angela's father hesitated before leaving. He said, "My other daughter is getting to know the kids on this block. Everywhere she goes she's popular. I'll get her to find out who did this and we'll put a stop to this nuisance. She's some kid, my Skipper. Do you know her?" Pride straightened his shoulders and strengthened his voice.

"It's this one I know. Angela, you want to see my garden, you come over. Anytime. I told you, Berman, she's a nice girl."

"Yes, of course."

"Daddy, c-can I? Mama told me no."

"You sure she won't be a trouble to you? No? Well, much obliged. I'll fix it up with her mother. If I can." Max Berman laughed weakly.

Kaminsky raised his hand in a good-bye gesture. He stood in his doorway a moment to watch Angela make her clumsy way across the street. Max Berman, he noticed, did not take her hand.

He fingered his doorbell, his heavy face sagging under the weight of his thoughts. He was about to go inside when he changed his mind. In a sudden gesture he closed his door behind him and ran down the few steps to his garden. There in the darkness he bent to his roses.

SEVEN

Angela's mother was at the sewing machine when her husband and daughter returned from their visit to Kaminsky. White linen cut and pinned with pattern paper was spread out over the dining room table.

Angela ran to her mother to watch the needle go up and down.

"What took you so long?" asked Mrs. Berman, biting off a thread. Mr. Berman checked his watch and said with surprise, "It's later than I thought. Well, we had a very interesting time."

His wife stopped the whirring of the machine to look at him with impatience. "So? What I want to know is, did you warn him about keeping away from Angela? Max, you're the limit. Your daughter was in that house with a couple of strange men, and you talk about interesting. What did you say to him? What excuse did he have?"

Angela leaned against her mother. A frown creased her forehead. "The b-bell kept ringing and ringing," she said. Mrs. Berman put a hand on her daughter's arm to hush her. "Yes, dear. Your father and I are talking."

"Ruth, you've got it all wrong. Roses is what it was all about. There was nobody else there. Only Mr. Kaminsky and he was doing her a favor. Her legs got scratched in his garden and he was fixing her up. Believe me, he didn't mean any harm."

Seeing her doubt, exasperation overtook him. "You do this to me all the time! Always seeing threats, when there aren't any. Always expecting the sky to fall down. I tell you it was embarrassing for me over there!"

He was pacing around the table as he spoke, not looking at his wife. When he did, he saw from the set of her lips that she was about to go off on one of her tirades. It was her suffering eyes that stopped him from saying more. They always managed to reach the pool of guilt dammed up inside him, a brimming reservoir called Angela. He knew everything his wife was going to say; they had been through this so many times before. It was like a dance they had to go through every once in a while, each one knowing the steps. He didn't want to dance, he was tired of it. For the sake of peace, he bent stiffly to kiss his wife's cheek. "I'm sorry, Ruthie, forget what I said. I know how hard it is for you, don't think I don't."

In a swift change of subject he said, "I want to talk to Skip. That Kaminsky has a little problem on his hands." He called to his daughter, going to the passageway and bellowing down the hallway with his loud hearty voice.

She was in her room pasting pictures of movie

stars in her scrapbook. On her desk was an open paste pot, a pair of scissors and *Photoplay* magazine. She had just cut out a picture of Gary Cooper, her current love. She wiped her sticky fingers on her bathrobe and stuck her head out of her door. "Yes, Dad?" she said eagerly, "What do you want?"

He was still mad at her as far as she could tell. All he had given her when he came home from work that evening was a peck on the cheek. No smile, no asking about her day. But her mother had started in on him right away, to go over to Kaminsky across the street on account of Angela. So she really couldn't tell what kind of mood he was in.

"Come here a minute, honey."

Honey! He wasn't angry anymore! Maybe her mother had told him what a good worker she had been all day. After Jean Persico's visit, Skip would have washed the floor with her tongue if her mother had asked. She was that happy.

Mrs. Berman clucked her tongue. "Tsk, that girl is supposed to be in bed. Don't keep her long, Max. You too, my darling," she said to Angela. "Go on to your room now. I'll be in there to tend to you soon."

"No! I don't want to." Angela knew how to get her own way with her mother.

Mrs. Berman gave in immediately. "Then stand up and I'll pin this dress on you. We'll see about the fitting."

Max Berman shook his head at this. Under his breath he muttered, "She spoils her," but said nothing.

Instead he fingered the material. He said, "I

thought you were making curtains for our bedroom."

"No, no, she needs dresses for school, though Lord knows she doesn't belong there. Stand still, child. I don't want to prick you."

Her husband looked at her with something like despair. He clasped his hands behind his head and looked up at the brass chandelier that spread its light over the table. His voice was strained but level as he said to her, "She doesn't belong there? Ruthie, we turned our life upside down so she could go to that school! We moved from one place to another so we could be close to it. I'm working an extra job to pay for it, and now all of a sudden she doesn't belong there?" His big good-natured face was sweaty with frustration.

Skip padded into the dining room sucking a finger. "Umm, paste tastes good, you know that?"

Her father's face brightened when she came in, as if a light switched on behind it. "Come here to me, Boopsie."

It was his baby name for her. She climbed onto his lap gratefully. He laid his cheek along the top of her head.

Her father said, "Well, Ruthie?"

Through the pins in her mouth she muttered, "Not now," and gestured with her head to her girls as if to say, not in front of the children.

He nodded and turned his attention to Skip. "You know the man across the street? Mr. Kaminsky?"

"Kaminsky, not mister," Angela corrected. She said the name as if she owned him.

"Yes. Kaminsky. Well, somebody played a mean trick on him tonight. Someone stuck a pin in his doorbell so that it wouldn't stop ringing."

Angela put her hands over her ears, distressed all over again. "It rang and rang!"

Her mother pulled her arms down. "Don't move around like that, lovey. I'm taking these pins out now."

Skip sat up and stared at her father. "I didn't do it!" she cried sharply, immediately defensive for no reason, except she felt uneasy.

In a flash she remembered Jean saying to Angela that afternoon that she had a joke for Kaminsky. And then it came to her with the thud of a heartbeat that once before Jean had hinted that she had fixed him. Those were her words.

Again she said to her father, "I didn't do it!" meaning *she* didn't.

"Well, of course you didn't! No, what I think is that it was the prank of some kid around here. They do things they think are funny and they don't realize. I know it sounds like nothing much but that man Kaminsky was badly shaken. He tried not to show it but he was. Odd reaction . . ."

"Is there a wife over there? Family?" Mrs. Berman was idly curious, more interested in fitting Angela.

"I didn't see a wife, but speaking of family, he has a whole bunch of pictures on the wall, all flowers that he names after people. His family, Angela called them; didn't you, my girl?"

Angela cupped her mother's face in her hands and said to her earnestly, "I n-named every one, Mama. Kaminsky's family. But not the no-name."

Mrs. Berman pressed her daughter's hand and then kissed it.

Her husband, gazing at his wife and child, said, as if handing her a gift, "Ruthie, he thinks Angela is good with flowers. He said some very nice things about her."

Mrs. Berman's cheeks flushed. Her lips pressed together in a pleased smile.

Max Berman drew Skip's head to his shoulder.

He said to her, "So, you are already getting to know some other children on the block. What I want you to do is to keep your ears open. If you get wind of who did this I want you to tell me. I feel obligated to that man."

Skip blinked up at the ceiling, thinking this over. "What would you do to them? . . . I mean, just supposing. What if I found out?"

"Do?" he chuckled into her hair. "I guess I would pay a little visit to the youngster's family. Let them take care of him. I don't want to have Kaminsky bothered, that's all. It's the least I can do. I told you. He was upset even though he didn't let on. Ruth, you remember that lady upstairs in our old apartment? The one who lost her daughter in a bicycle accident? That's who he reminded me of. The same look in the eyes. Haunted. Know what I mean?"

His wife nodded and they exchanged a companionable glance. He set Skip on her feet. "Okay everybody, off to bed." He clapped his hands together as if chasing away stray animals, "Shoo now. Scat!"

Mrs. Berman called after Angela, "I'll be in in a second."

When their children were gone, Max Berman sat

across the table from his wife. He cleared away a space for his elbows and said, "Well?"

"Well what?" Mrs. Berman didn't raise her head from her sewing. Her bottom lip was caught between her teeth as if to hold back a tide.

He said reasonably, "Look, Ruthie, don't give me that. We have to talk about this. We move from our old apartment in the city where the commute is easy for me and we set down here in the backstreets of the Bronx. Why? So Angela can have the benefit of this school. Okay, okay, I was willing to do that. I take on an extra job, right? After a day's work at the plant I do the books for some lousy stationery store to pay for it."

He stood and leaned toward her with his knuckles on the table, his voice strained. "Did I complain? You bet your sweet life I didn't. You had your hopes up again and I would turn myself inside out if I thought it would help Angie's future. But I'll be damned if I'll do it for nothing! Now what did you mean by her not belonging there?"

Mrs. Berman's head shot up. "You did! You did complain! I knew what you were thinking. Always the pessimist, always putting her down, always pressing her and pushing her! You didn't believe in that school from the beginning."

This made him close his eyes for a moment as if praying for patience. "Will you stick to the subject for once, woman! What does that have to do with what I'm asking? What's going to happen to her if I don't push and prod? What's her future? You think I'm going to be here forever? You think giving in to her every wish will make up to her for what she doesn't have? You think your dresses will make a difference? Help her get a job?" He swept away the material on the table violently. "Not even that school can do that. I'll work like a horse to send her there but then what? Who hires the Angelas of this lousy world!"

"Don't raise your voice to me! A job!" She spat that out like a dirty word. "Don't forget, Angela has a mother and a sister. She doesn't need a job. We'll take care of her. For your information, I'll tell you why she's too good for that place. She's much better than anyone I saw in the halls, Mr. Pessimist."

She rose from her chair and clutched her sewing to her breast. Passionately she said, "You should have seen how she worked in the house with me today. She fixed the linen closet better than I could. She straightened and washed the kitchen cabinets better than a professional. That's all I meant. She's smarter than anyone gives her credit for. I'm the only one who knows. Oh, she'll go to the school, all right. She'll show them."

At that, a certain change in her took place. It was in her eyes and in the lift of her chin. Max Berman groaned at the sight. He had seen hope raised and dashed too many times.

His wife sat and smoothed out her sewing on the table. "Maybe she can teach there someday. Sure, why not?"

Mr. Berman slumped in his chair as if a hand had shoved him there. He muttered, "What to do? Too good for the school, not good enough for life. Slipped through the cracks." His face bent to his chest. He rubbed his temples in a circular movement as if easing a headache.

Skip heard the angry voices coming from the dining room. Angela was in her room with her looking at the scrapbook. She had begged to see it before going to bed.

Skip left her sister there and slipped into the dark hallway so she could hear better.

She stood on one foot and leaned against the wall. Her short nightdress stuck to her in the sweaty rush of fear these fights between her parents always aroused. She listened.

Her father said, in a way that made her see plainly his staring eyes and the outraged look on his face, "What do you mean, she has a sister to take care of her? Now you listen to me. We are not saddling that child with Angela all her life! She's our responsibility, not hers. Skip has her own life to live. I won't have it, you hear me?"

Mrs. Berman's voice shook with emotion. "What won't you have? We're a family. Angela is Skip's family. You can't get away from that!"

"No, but that doesn't mean she's her burden!"

Skip, hearing her own name, whimpered.

It seemed to her that she had been hearing the same fight forever. All her life she had heard those voices rise against one another over Angela. All her life she had pulled the covers over her head, or stuffed her fingers in her ears, or ran into the bathroom so as not to hear their anger at one another. Now that she was older she still couldn't bear the terrible anger, but at the same time she couldn't leave. She was impelled to listen, held there as if it were somehow her fault or that it was up to her to make it better.

There was a lull in the voices from the dining room. Skip found she had been holding her breath. She let it out carefully, and wiped her forehead with her arm. Then she tiptoed back to her room.

Angela was busy cutting out pictures she had found in the magazine while Skip was gone. They were all pictures of flowers. Paste smeared the table and pages of the scrapbook. Paste coated her fingers and dabbed her face.

Angela was pleased with herself. She said to her sister, "L-look what I did. I have my family here too, just like Kaminsky. See these ones? They are all Skips. The flowers the lady is holding, are called M-Mamas. I have to f-find Daddy flowers."

Skip saw the damage to her scrapbook and it felt as if the damage were to her own body. All that was pent up in her as she listened in the hallway welled up and out. From her open throat rose a shrill screech that began in her toes. Angela dropped the book in shock.

All Skip knew at the moment was that her sister was the cause of all the trouble in the house. Whenever her mother cried it was over Angela. Whenever her mother and father had a fight it was over her. She made everybody crazy. Skip couldn't do this, couldn't do that, couldn't breathe because of her sister. And now this. She couldn't stand it one single second more. She wanted her dead.

"I hate you!" she screamed. "I hate you!" came from the bottom of her heart. She pushed over Angela's chair in a single furious movement. Angela sprawled on the floor bellowing more with fright than hurt.

Mr. and Mrs. Berman burst into the room as Skip was still shouting. She was stopped by a slap in the face from her mother. Skip, crying afresh, ran to her father's arms, as Mrs. Berman tended to Angela.

Mr. and Mrs. Berman faced one another as if from across an impassable river, each holding and comforting a child.

EIGHT

At ten o'clock on Thursday morning, Skip stood squinting in the morning sun outside her doorway. The muggy heat had been swept away by a rainstorm the night before. A fresh breeze lifted her hair, its cool edge hinting at the coming of autumn. Her punishment was over and she was free.

As she remained for a moment breathing in the street, smells of dirt and tar and various cooking odors, she wasn't aware of the constant smile that lit her face.

The street was still quiet at that hour, basking in the sun as if storing up energy for later. Mothers were out food shopping and many had taken their children with them. Across the street Kaminsky's solitary figure could be seen already at work in his garden. A few kids were hanging around the fire hydrant. Up the block the bratty red-headed twins had broken up a hopscotch game, throwing the potzie to one another over the heads of three screaming little girls. Their cries punctuated the morning air like scolding birds.

Skip had on her favorite short shorts and her father's old red striped shirt rescued from the give-away bag. Her mother and sister were going to be out shopping most of the day. Jean had said to call for her this morning. They would go together to the clubroom. The day was beautiful and it was all hers.

Skip felt just fine.

Her long bare legs tingled to get moving. She jogged across the street to Jean Persico's house and pressed the doorbell.

Jean had paid daily visits to her while she was grounded. She had stood in the alley under her window to report what the club had done that day. Mostly they had cleaned the room and decided on the name.

"We're The Dares," Jean had told her. "Know why? We dared to go in that house, we dared to open that door. It just hit me when I woke up this morning. We can dare to do anything we want. We're The Dares!"

Skip had agreed that it was a terrific name. The idea, as she understood it, was that being in the club meant that they would dare one another to do things. Risky things.

Her stomach lurched when she heard this. She had already done a risky thing and had gotten three days punishment for it. Two risky things as a matter of fact: leaving her sister and breaking into an abandoned house. But there was no turning back now. She would rather die than not be with Jean Persico and in the club.

While Skip waited on the porch for her friend to appear, she peered inside one of the windows. The shades were drawn halfway down so she had to stoop to peer in.

She decided it must be the living room she was seeing because there was a couch with shiny pillows against the opposite wall. Above it hung a statue of Jesus. It was too dark in there to see much else.

Skip rang the doorbell once more and knocked on the door for good measure. It could only be exciting and wonderful inside the house because Jean lived there. She would take a good look around once she was inside, save it up to think about in bed tonight.

The most mysterious and unimaginable fact about Jean Persico was that she had no mother. Skip had learned this in one of her alley visits.

"Won't your mother mind?" This was Skip's automatic question when Jean had mentioned that she had taken a vacuum cleaner to the clubroom.

"No, she's dead."

That was all Jean said about it and Skip was too awed to ask how come. She also found out that her friend lived in this house with two older brothers and a father.

If Jean had told her that she had been raised by bears or gypsies it wouldn't have seemed any more odd or exotic than to be the only girl in a house of grown-up men. Jean had told her how wonderful her brothers were to her, always giving her things to wear and taking her to the movies. Skip imagined that they treated her like a favorite doll, like the dwarfs treated Snow White.

The door opened while she was still looking through the window.

Jean Persico stuck her head out. She had on a blue striped apron so large it brushed her sneakers. When she saw who it was she said, "Hey, gimme a minute."

Skip grinned and said "Sure," moving to wait inside.

Jean stopped her. "You wait here," she said. "I'll be right out."

The door closed, leaving Skip staring at it, disappointed, straining to hear the voices inside. There was some yelling.

Moments later, when Jean emerged, she was wearing the same torn sundress she always did. She stormed past Skip without speaking, jumped down the porch steps in one go and ran to the corner without stopping. Skip caught up with her in front of Abchek's grocery.

Jean hung an arm around her neck and panted in her ear, "Wait till you hear what I thought of for an initiation. Perfect for antsy Francey." She could hardly speak for laughing at some inner joke. Whatever had gone on in her house she had left behind.

"Initiation?"

"Sure. What do you think? To get into this club, first you have to do a terrific dare, like an initiation. Today's the day, everybody knows that. Hey, race you to the room."

To be out of the house for the first time in days and running free with her idol was close to heaven for Skip. As she ran, Skip pictured what the secret room would look like now that it was fixed up. She imagined drapes and incense, a den, a place of voodoo.

Instead, when the two of them burst in, what

struck her mostly was the light pouring in from the washed windows. The floor had been swept clean, and the old chair was now in the center of the room.

Francine and Norma grinned hello like old friends. Another girl was with them. Skip had seen her occasionally with Jean Persico in the days when she was just a watcher.

The girls were sitting on the floor, grouped around the old dilapidated chair as if it were a throne, reserved for royalty.

Jean went immediately to the chair. It was taken for granted by everybody that she belonged there.

Skip said Hi to everybody and sat cross-legged between Norma and the new girl. Francine, on the other side of Norma, was concentrating on her chocolate licorice, tearing off bites and chewing the rubbery candy as if it were her last meal.

The new girl, who was introduced as Ellie, said, "Hi. I saw you move in from my bedroom window. I was playing sick that day."

"You can get away with that?" Skip's mother would know in a minute.

"Yeah." Ellie had long reddish hair, a spatter of freckles across a bony nose and smelled of cough drops. Her nostrils were pink and so were the rims of her eyes under the straw lashes. Used Kleenexes were in her lap. When she smiled at Skip her teeth seemed too big for her face. It was a good smile, full of braces and friendliness.

Jean hushed them, crackling with impatience. She was full of something to say.

"Okay, okay, shut up everybody, we already chose,

so Francine goes first. Initiation time, right, Francey?"

Francine stopped chewing and then swallowed in a gulp. "I say let's choose over again. It's not fair if Skip wasn't here. Maybe she'd have to do the first dare, not me. How do we know?"

Jean broke into an assured and blinding smile. "Francey, you're gonna love it!" She sprang from her chair to go to the window. A line of electricity seemed to flow from her to the other girls. They watched her movements as if plugged into her.

She leaned out of the open window and looked down to the courtyard. When she turned back to the waiting girls she was gleeful, hardly able to get the words out. Pointing to Francine she intoned, "In the name of The Dares . . . No, here's how it goes: We, the future members of the Dare Club, dare Francine Gluvis to put . . ."

Here she broke down, and the rest tumbled out in a rush. ". . . To put a cockroach in the ice cream at LoPatti's drugstore!"

She was prevented from saying more by screams and squeals. It went over big.

"Wait a minute. Wait a minute. I'm not finished yet! Then Francine . . ." Jean had to stop for control. "Francine has to make a big thing of it out loud. You know, say like, 'Hey, what's this! What kind of place is this with cockroaches?'"

Skip was enraptured. She was on her feet in one movement. "You can scream! Or faint maybe. How about that?"

It was Ellie who screamed. She pointed to the air in front of her with her eyes bulging with horror and a hand at her breast. "A roach!" she cried, "I'm going to puke!" She pantomimed doing so with first-rate sound effects.

By this time even Francine was laughing.

Jean had to admire Ellie's performance. "Yeah, like that," she instructed Francine. "Okay? That's your dare. Otherwise you're out of the club."

"Okay, okay. Right now, you mean? Who has a cockroach for me? Eeek. I have to put that thing in good ice cream?" That seemed to be the worst of it for Francine. She added, "I tell you what. I'm going to run out right after, and you all better be right there."

They all gabbled their assurance. Skip pointed out that how would they know she did it if they weren't right there? A general hilarity had taken hold of them all. They were silly with anticipation.

Jean even had the answer for where to find the necessary roach. "In the garbage," she said, pointing out the window. "In the backyard. I saw plenty there last time. That's what gave me the idea. Come on, everybody. Let's go."

They ran downstairs and out to the yard where, sure enough, there were roaches crawling over the rotting rinds and skins of unidentifiable things. With sticks in hand they rooted around making pretend retching noises. It was Norma who had to give up. For her, the pretend noises were about to turn into the real thing.

"Quick, give me a box, somebody!" demanded Jean, holding up her stick. A large brown roach crawled at the tip, its feelers exploring the air.

Box? Box? Nobody had thought of what to put it in.

Ellie said, "I got one." She emptied her cough drops into the pocket of her plaid shorts and held out the empty box. Jean shook the bug from her stick. It was inside, and captive, ready for Francine.

LoPatti's drugstore was on the opposite corner from Abchek's grocery. Mrs. LoPatti waited on the ice cream counter, while her white-coated husband, a half-head shorter and a hundred pounds lighter, took care of the pharmacy department.

The girls of the Dare Club crowded outside the store, shading their eyes in the bright sun to peer in through the windows. Behind them the street was now in high gear, full of noise and movement.

Francine clutched the box. Close to noon on a beautiful August morning there were three women in hats and a crying child sitting at the counter. The little boy was pointing to one of the jars of penny candy in front of him, wailing for what he couldn't have. There was an empty stool between two of the ladies.

"Go on, go on in," prodded several fingers in her back.

"Wait a minute," said Francine turning to them with something like relief. "I can't. We forgot one thing."

"What?"

"Money," she declared. "How am I supposed to order ice cream without money?"

The rest of them looked at one another with dismay. It hadn't occurred to them.

None of them had any. Skip thought of the jar behind the cereal boxes where her mother kept some change, but then she realized that was in the other apartment. Maybe her mother kept it in the same place here but she didn't volunteer to search. She wasn't about to look for more trouble.

Jean said in a wheedling way, "Ellie, you can always get some. How about it? Go ask your mother. Please? Pretty please?"

"I don't have to ask. I have some in my sock drawer. What do we need? A dime?"

Francine was firm. "Fifteen cents. If I'm going to do this I'm going to get a sundae. Hot fudge." She licked her upper lip as if she could already taste it.

Ellie dashed away, and while they waited they planned what Francine should do.

As they spoke, Skip kept an eye on the all-important empty stool inside, worried that somebody might take it. LoPatti's was a busy place. People kept going in and out, but mostly for ice cream cones or medicine. The seat remained empty. Every time the screen door opened, the sweet cool smell of ice creams and syrups reached the group of girls. They would pause and turn their faces to the wonderful smell like roses to the sun.

Skip swallowed saliva, and ran in place to use up energy. Waiting was always hard for her. Occasional giggles spilled from her at what they were planning, and spread like measles to the others.

It was agreed that Francine could eat almost all of the sundae. She held out strongly for this point. When Mrs. LoPatti wasn't looking, she was to shake the box and drop the cockroach into what was left in the dish. Then she had to scream. The scream was important so that the other people in the store would see the bug. The LoPattis would have a fit.

"Okay, okay, I know what to do." Francine had heard enough. She was getting more and more nervous and at the same time she wanted the ice cream. "I'm going to act real shook up, you'll see. Hey, I'll ask for my money back. How's that!" She was so proud of thinking that up all by herself that when Ellie returned, she nodded confidently at their encouragement, opened the screen door and walked into the drugstore.

The girls lined up to watch through the glass window.

Francine climbed up on the high stool at the counter between the two women. The girls outside saw her give her order to Mrs. LoPatti. While her sundae was being made, Francine turned to the window and held up the cockroach box. She waved it at them and pretended to kiss it.

Mrs. LoPatti put the dish of ice cream before her with a polite business smile on her broad rouged face. Francine pointed to the sundae and said something to her. The smile was dropped. Mrs. LoPatti sprinkled another spoonful of nuts over the cherry, atop the mound of whipped cream, above the ice cream, covered with warm thick chocolate syrup.

The watchers groaned as one at this sight.

Francine seemed to believe in separate but equal time for all. First, the cherry was carefully placed to one side, to be saved for last. The nuts were scraped to a happy death at the bottom of the dish, drowned in fudge. She then spent a year or so, spooning up whipped cream, untainted by any hint of nut or chocolate. Her tongue seemed to linger at the spoon forever, darting in and out like a cat's. When that was done she was ready for serious business—the right, the exquisite, mixture of hot fudge and ice cream.

The girls outside were following each spoonful on its long trip. Skip had never seen anyone give such complete attention to something to eat, or do it with such finesse. It reminded her of the way her Uncle Reub ate a lobster.

"Come on! Come on!" egged on her cheering section.

Jean clapped a hand to her forehead. "That roach is going to die of starvation first."

Skip said, "Wait, wait. She just ate the cherry! She's getting ready. She's taking out the box. She's going to do it!"

Mrs. LoPatti had her back turned to the counter. Francine took the box from her lap, and shook it over the ice cream dish. Skip saw her look down into the dish and then peer into the box. As plain as if she had spoken, Francine was saying, "Where is that thing?" Again she shook the box over her dish. No cockroach.

By now, Francine was so absorbed she didn't notice that she had attracted the attention of the women on each side of her. They were watching this queer exercise with a great deal of curiosity.

So was Mrs. LoPatti.

Just then, after a particularly hard shake, the stubborn roach was finally dislodged. It was sent flying, not in Francine's dish, but on the counter where it began to make itself at home right under Mrs. LoPatti's nose.

For a big woman she was a fast mover. With a cry

of outrage that reached the spellbound girls outside and way beyond, she pounced. The bug was squashed in a paper napkin while Francine was still trying to locate it in her ice cream dish.

Mrs. LoPatti stretched out an arm and pointed to the door like a crossing guard. "Out!" she ordered Francine, who dashed out the door as if she had robbed the safe.

The girls outside took that as an order too. They streamed away from the drugstore, running for cover the way roaches do under siege.

NINE

High up in the tree Norma was stuck. She clung to the branch for dear life. It was a tall maple shaped like an umbrella in back of Ellie's house. Its limbs were perfect for climbing. She was halfway to the top when she made the mistake of looking down at her friends on the ground. When she saw how high she was, she froze, unable to move an inch.

"I can't!" she wailed.

The other members of the Dare Club were grouped around the trunk of the tree looking up at the terrified girl. It was Monday, midmorning, a few days after Francine's roach dare. This time it was Norma carrying out the challenge given her by Jean Persico.

Skip had an urge to shinny up the tree that minute and get Norma down. She could do it in nothing flat. Climbing a tree like this was a cinch and yet when Norma was told what her initiation was to be, she had carried on like it was Mount Everest.

To Skip it was another proof of Jean Persico's genius that she knew just what was the hardest thing for each of them to do. She had told Skip that her dare was next. Her stomach did somersaults at the thought. One thing was sure: her dare wasn't going to be easy like Norma's.

Skip put her hand on the light brown trunk and fixed her eyes on the scared girl trying to send up confidence.

Standing next to her and a half head shorter was Ellie, who sneezed and sprayed the bark. She blew her nose and put the soggy tissue into the pocket of her shorts, where it had plenty of company. "You knew she was afraid of heights!" she accused Jean Persico, whose back was against the trunk of the tree, her face looking up through the branches.

"Sure I knew. What's the point of a dare if it's easy?"

Skip agreed with Jean, but looked down at Ellie with a tinge of awe. It took nerve to stand up to Jean, nerve she didn't think she had but somehow Ellie did.

Francine shouted up to Norma. "There's a branch right under your foot. What are you so scared of? It's right there!" She had passed her own initiation to the club and was quite keen to advise the less fortunate.

"Save your breath," Jean told her. "She's stuck up there. Maybe what we need is a rope. We could throw it up to her."

"Or a ladder," said Ellie. "Except we don't have one long enough."

"How about if I climb up there with her?" offered Skip. "I can do it easy. I'll hang on to her and get her down."

Jean called up to Norma, "Skip's coming up. Hang on."

"No!" screamed Norma. "Nobody touch me. I'll fall. Mama!" She was straddling a branch, lying along its length, clutching it to her like a drowning person. The girls on the ground could see her body, but her face was hidden by the leaves. They could hear her. They all heard the hysteria.

Skip jumped up on the trunk of the tree, clasping it between her strong legs, about to climb to the thick leafy branch above her. She was going after Norma no matter what.

Her action made the tree shake a bit. Norma, feeling the tremor, shrieked with fear. "No! No!" She shrilled on that one note until Skip jumped down.

Skip gave up when she heard Norma scream like that. It dawned on her that maybe they wouldn't be able to get the girl down.

They were all getting very nervous. Jean circled the trunk of the tree, peering up through the leaves at the terrified girl who was glued to the branch like a fungus.

She suddenly slapped the bark of the tree as if it were the tree's fault that things were going wrong.

"Stop looking at me like that!" she said to the other girls. "I'm not the only one here. I'm not going to take the blame. One of you guys think of something. Not just me all the time!"

Skip said doubtfully, "Maybe we should get her mother."

Francine was definite. "Forget it. Nobody's home in her house. Her mother's divorced. She works." She shouted up at Norma in sudden fury, "Norma Brandon, you stop fooling around and come on down!"

The girls stood at the foot of the tree, their faces upturned, still as statues. Skip held her breath, waiting to see if this got results. The only sound from the trapped girl was an animal whimper. Pure terror.

After a few moments of this Ellie announced, "Well, my mother is home and I'm getting her and nobody's going to stop me. You guys wait here."

Her house was one of the larger ones at the circle of the dead-end street. The tree was behind it in a corner of the small cemented backyard near the garage. Its branches reached across the yard and shaded the shingled roof. The branch that Norma clung to was almost as high as the roof.

As Ellie skipped away, heading for the back door of her house, Jean yelled to her, "Don't you tell on us!"

Ellie stopped walking and just stared at her with a fist on her hip. Skip saw Jean stare back, her hazel eyes blazing. Uh-oh, said Skip to herself. In her geography book there was a picture of two deer locking horns. It was that picture that rose to her mind now. Instead of a clash of antlers, Ellie shrugged and disappeared through the back door of her house.

A minute or two later, an upstairs window opened and Mrs. Lefcourt, Ellie's mother, leaned out. She called to the girl in the tree. "Norma Brandon, come down from there at once!"

"Owww. Get me dowwwwwn."

Ellie poked her head out alongside her mother's. "I told you. She's stuck up there. She won't move."

Mrs. Lefcourt called to Norma, "Hold on, hold on. We'll get you down."

Mrs. Lefcourt had a habit of talking to herself,

passing out advice as she would to any needy stranger. She closed the window and said, "Now don't get excited. Just keep calm. It won't do a bit of good to excite yourself. Oh me oh my, now think. What to do?" She twisted her string of beads as she looked off at nothing in particular. Patches of red lay on her cheeks like clumsy rouge. She was thinking, taking her own advice.

Ellie sneezed. This diverted her mother from one crisis to another. "I knew it! This is too much for you!" she cried. Her hand immediately went to her daughter's forehead to feel for fever.

"No, no, I'm fine, go on, what should we do?"

Her mother said, "I'm calling the fire department! If they can get cats down, they can get Norma. Whatever possessed that child to climb up there!"

It wasn't a question Ellie was about to answer. She left her mother on the phone to race outside with the news.

First she called up to Norma, "It's okay. My mother knows what to do. Just hang on."

No response from Norma. Not a leaf moved on her branch. She was so still she could have been asleep.

"Maybe she fainted," whispered Francine. That was too awful to comment on. Skip pictured Norma letting go, bouncing downward from one branch to another until the tree spilled her onto the ground where she broke like a dish.

When Ellie told the girls that her mother called the fire department, Jean exploded. "Oh great! Now you did it. The whole world is going to know how come she's up there. We get the blame!"

This made the girls more frightened than Norma was, up in the tree.

"I'm sorry," whispered Ellie, entirely deflated.

"What will they do to us?" Francine whimpered.

Jail. Skip could only think of her father's face when the judge sentenced her. What she wanted to do at that moment was to run and hide.

Automatically they looked to Jean to decide what to do. "Okay, okay," she said, circling the tree, biting her lip, planning their next move. A few seconds of this and she was ready. "We don't know anything about this," she told them. "We're going to get out of here and spread, everybody home. If they ask us, we lie. Okay? Let's go!"

Too late. The sound of the fire siren stopped them cold. It was out front. They moved close to one another for comfort, standing in a solemn row as heavy feet pounded down the alley.

Nobody paid any attention to them. They could have run but they didn't. It was all too fascinating and went too fast. In a matter of an eyeblink, or so it seemed to Skip, the ladder was raised and one of the firemen raced up. Down he came with a sack slung over his shoulder that was Norma.

He set the girl on her feet and squatted in front of her, making sure she was all right. Norma's face was chalk white and bits of bark clung to her runny nose and wet face. Other than having been scared to death she was all right.

Two other firemen swiftly gathered up the ladder. After an irritated glance at snuffling Norma, they returned it to the fire engine.

Mrs. Lefcourt had watched the rescue from the upstairs window. When it was over, she shouted to the men, "Yoo-hoo down there. Thank you, thank you very much."

The fireman who had carried Norma down the ladder looked up and said, "Is this your child, ma'am?"

"Dear me, no. My own girl is over there. She's the one who told me of Norma's plight. Say hello, Ellie."

The fireman frowned at the clump of girls. Ellie waggled her fingers at him. As he strode over to them, Jean muttered, "Remember, we don't know anything." Four girls stared up at him with round eyes, waiting to be taken away in handcuffs.

The fireman said to Ellie, "You the one who spotted her? She wouldn't have held on much longer. Nice work."

They stared at him blankly. They hadn't expected congratulations.

Jean Persico recovered first. She said, "Well, actually, I was the one. I was walking by and I heard this yell, you know? So I saw her up there and, boy, was I worried. I got ahold of Ellie and then . . ."

Ellie interrupted her. She put a hand on the fireman's sleeve, looked up into his eyes and said earnestly, "And then I called her other friends. These here. Because I knew what Norma was trying to do. We all do, don't we girls?" Skip was too enthralled to nod.

Ellie confided to the man, "Her father was killed in the war. Her mother has to go out begging in the streets. She's alone all the time. No wonder she climbs a tree to get away from it all." She whispered, "Who knows what she was thinking of up there? I don't want to say it!" She shuddered.

The firefighter stood up, his ruddy honest face shocked. "Look here kid, what are you telling me? You talking suicide? Is that what it was?" This changed everything. He fished in his pocket for a notebook. "What's your name? Norma what?"

Skip jumped in. She just opened her mouth and out came, "Oh hey, Ellie was just talking, you know. Kidding around. Weren't you, Ellie?" She loved the story but things were getting out of hand.

Jean took over, whipping a scathing glance at Ellie. "Yeah, kidding around. Don't mind her. Norma here is a good friend of ours. She's okay. She likes to climb trees, is all. Maybe she got dizzy up there, who knows? She just doesn't say much, do you, Norm? Just tell him you're okay."

She squeezed Norma's hand as she spoke but if it was a warning not to talk, Norma didn't need it. She was hardly there. She was leaning her weight against Jean, just able to mumble to the puzzled fireman that she was all right. The yawning pit that had opened in her stomach when she was up so high had not entirely closed over. She might still fall, might still vomit.

The fireman said, "What? Well, you're sure?" He scowled suspiciously at Ellie, and then turned back to Norma. "Okay, now you better thank these friends of yours. Lucky for you they were here. And don't go climbing trees anymore. For any reason. You understand? We got better things to do down at the station."

He nodded to them and left.

The girls stared after him. When they were sure he was gone they broke out into wild laughter, pounding one another. They raced around the yard while Norma recovered. After a while they all ran out to the street, stopping at Skip's house to sprawl on the steps and catch their breath.

Skip was reviewing the scene in her head as she panted. No jail, no trouble, they had gotten away scot-free. She was with the best friends of her whole life.

Mrs. Berman bustled out of the house. "Did you hear those fire engines?" she asked the girls with some excitement. "They were right down the street. Someone told me it was a false alarm."

Angela was with her. "Fire," she said and put her hands over her ears as she mimicked the sound of the siren.

Jean said with a straight face, "Fire engine? We were all in my house. Guess we didn't hear it."

Skip's mother beamed at them all as their laughter broke around her. Jean's remark was all the funnier since they all knew she never asked anyone inside. Mrs. Berman didn't care what they were laughing at. What she saw stretched out on her steps was opportunity. Her Angela could be with the girls for a while. For as long as it lasted she could see her daughter sitting among them, just another girl, one of the bunch.

"Stay, Angela. Stay here with your sister and these nice friends."

Skip was too far gone in ecstasy to mind her sister's presence.

Norma, fully recovered now, took up Jean's hand

and twined it with her own. In her childish way, as if getting around her mother, she asked, "So am I in? Huh, Jean? I almost died in that tree. I went up it, didn't I? Don't I get in the club for that? Francine is in and she didn't get the cockroach in the ice cream."

"Nope," said Jean.

"Why not?" Norma was tearing up again.

"Because, crybaby, you didn't do your dare, did she, girls?"

Francine as always was the first to agree with Jean.

Ellie didn't answer. Skip was hesitating because Norma had a point. Should she say so?

Jean Persico didn't count votes. "There," she said. "Everybody agrees with me so forget it. You almost got us in trouble. Lucky for us I told off that fireman."

"Hey!" protested Ellie, poking Skip.

Jean had something else on her mind. Her bold eyes were fixed across the street where Kaminsky's flowers bobbed in the occasional breeze.

Suddenly a secretive smile lifted her chapped lips as she said to Norma, "Don't worry. You'll get in. I have an easy one for you this time." Her smile now was so full of mischief that something quickened in the girls. The very air seemed more exciting to breathe.

TEN

Jean Persico had everyone's rapt attention and she let them wait. She pulled her dress away from her body and flapped it against her to stir up some air. "Whew, it's hot," she said, grinning at her audience on the steps.

It was such a hot day that the tar in the street was melting. Children were pulling it up, chewing it like gum. An open fire hydrant gushed across the street. The firemen had opened it up for the yelling, begging kids before they went back to the station. Some children had run home for bathing suits, some didn't bother to change. It didn't matter what they wore. It was a broiling August day and the water was on! Nothing was better than that. The street was full of children's cries as they pushed and ran in and out of the cold water from the hydrant shrieking their pleasure.

Skip watched a rainbow arch in the spray, jittery with curiosity about what was in store for Norma. She wished she could shake it out of Jean like salt.

Finally Jean said, "Okay, now listen. See that

place across the street?" She was pointing out Kaminsky's garden to Norma.

Angela followed Jean's finger. "Kaminsky!" she crowed. She knew whose place that was.

Jean said, "That's right," as Skip cried, "Shush."

"So what about it?" said Norma suspiciously. "All he does is yell. I'm afraid of that old guy."

"Yeah? Well don't be. Remember how he yelled at me? Did that hurt me? Names don't hurt. But now we're going to pay him back. All we need is a pin."

Skip's head snapped away from the garden back to Jean. Her father had talked about a pin.

"A pin?" repeated Norma.

"Yeah. If you want to be in the club you're going to stick it in his doorbell so it keeps on ringing. See? I told you it was easy."

Angela put her hands over her ears. "It kept on ringing and ringing."

Skip's heart was thudding. She knew what Angela was talking about and knew what was coming.

Jean was just warming up. She was tickled with herself, her force carrying everyone along with her like a tide. "Skip, get us a pin, okay? Your ma must have some around. It'll be fun, Norma, you'll see. I'll tell you how. There's nothing to it. Any baby can do it, even Angela here."

Francine giggled loudly at this. She was on the top step with Jean just below her, leaning against her knees. A satisfied look sat on her plump face because she was the one Jean was leaning against.

Angela was busy examining the freckles on Ellie's arm. She heard her name, looked up and smiled her sweet smile. She wasn't following the conversation.

Ellie put her arm across Angela's lap so the girl could look at it closer. She said to Jean, "How do you know it works?" She shook her red head doubtfully. "Suppose Norma is fooling around outside his door and Kaminsky catches her?"

Norma was all for that. "Yeah? What then?"

Skip had nothing to say because she knew why Jean was so sure this would work. She had done it before.

"Listen, it's a cinch!" Jean sat up straight and held out a hand as if knowing they were slipping away. "Hey, I've done it myself, I tell you. A couple of times."

She looked around, satisfied at the impression that made. They were with her again. Even Angela was listening now, nodding her head, looking from her to Kaminsky's house and back again, her mouth in an O of wonder.

Jean returned to Francine's legs. Leaning back carelessly she said, "Sure I did. You all heard him yell. Well, nobody yells at me. Nobody pushes me around. So . . . it was a lot of fun. You get the bell ringing and then you beat it. You don't hang around and wait for him, you dope." This was said laughingly to Norma.

She leaned forward again, drawing them in. "Hey listen, this is going to be fun. It happened so many times he'll think it's ghosts, like he's haunted! Serves him right. We'll fix him good."

Skip wished at that moment that she were up in Norma's tree. Or in bed fast asleep. She wished she were anyplace but here listening to Jean Persico tell how she played that trick on Kaminsky. Her father said she should find out who did it and now she knew, for sure. Her father wanted her to tell on her best friend, but she couldn't. She wouldn't.

Jean cried aloud, "Let's do it!" and it was like a bugle call to the girls on the steps. They leaned toward her like sunflowers. They nodded and poked one another, squealing their yesses, swept up by Jean's pull and the lure of mischief.

Even Skip, who a moment ago was in a stew, now found herself full of yes. Yes it was cruel, yes he was an old man, yes it was wrong to pester him. Yes, yes, yes there was a wildness here and yes she would do it. She could do anything. She didn't know that about herself until now, until Jean. It made her feel enlarged, as if her skin was expanding to make room for this new person.

Her mother came out to see what the noise was about. She wiped her hands on a dishtowel tied around her waist.

"Just checking to see what all the noise was about," she said, tucking stray hairs in her tumbling bun and smiling at them all. She squinted up at the sun stamped like a penny in the sky, and fanned the towel toward her face.

"Sure is hot. Would anyone care for something cool to drink?" she offered. "Lemonade? A Coke? Dr Pepper, maybe? Skip, get your friends something. Do you have to go to the bathroom, Angela honey?"

Skip felt more than heard the titters of her friends. She shot her sister a look of pure hatred. Bam, slice, bang. Angela was in little pieces all over the steps.

Jean Persico looked up at Skip's mother with a Sunday smile and said to her, "Do you have a pin,

Mrs. Berman? See? My hem here is down on this side. I want to pin it up till I get home."

Mrs. Berman took in the torn dress which needed more than a pin for the hem. She delved into a pocket of her housedress and pulled out a safety pin. "I think this will be better," she said. "I can get you a straight pin, but I think until your mother sews this up, a safety will hold it better. Does she have a sewing machine?"

"Oh, I don't have a mother. She died on account of me when I was born." Jean lowered her eyes and waited. It always worked on grownups.

Sure enough, Mrs. Berman was all sympathy. "You poor thing. Well, here, would you like me to run it up? It won't take but a second."

"No thanks," said Jean holding out her hand. "The pin will do fine."

When Mrs. Berman left them, Jean held the pin aloft and cried, "Aha! The murder weapon." She handed it to Norma. "Now here's what you do."

She told Norma how to wedge the pin between the bell button and the metal ring so that the button stayed down. "When I did it to him the other times I used a straight one but this will work just as well. When the bell starts ringing you get out of there quick, got it?"

Angela looked across the street to the roses. "It kept ringing and ringing."

As Norma took the pin, Ellie said, "Hey, wait a minute. I don't know. He's just an old guy."

Jean scoffed, "It's nothing. It's not hurting him any, a little pin in his door. And anyway, who cares? It's just for fun. Go on, Norma. We double dare you."

Francine repeated, "Go on, we dare you."

Norma had started across the street. The other girls ran to the side of Skip's house to see without being seen.

They left Angela on the steps. She watched Norma go toward Kaminsky's roses and stood up as if she meant to follow her.

"Sit down!" hissed Skip, and Angela did.

At Kaminsky's door Norma was fumbling with the pin. Skip reported every move to the girls behind her. Any moment she expected to see the door open and Kaminsky find Norma there messing around with that telltale pin in her hand.

Jean pushed her aside to look for herself. "Wait, wait, I think she's . . . There! She did it!"

The constant buzz carried to the hiding girls.

"Run, you dope, run!" muttered Jean.

As if she heard this Norma flew down the steps and ran back across the street to her friends.

Kaminsky opened his door and they crouched farther down against the house, not daring to even peek. The sound of the buzzer went on and on.

Skip couldn't wait. She had to poke her head out for an instant. It was long enough to make her heart sink.

Angela had crossed the street to Kaminsky after all.

There she was in front of his house looking up at him while he searched the street, turning his gray mop this way and that. Skip saw him raise his hands to his head. He wrenched the pin from the doorbell. The buzzing stopped. Angela was talking to him.

Skip saw him hold up the pin to her. He was asking her something.

"My sister's over there!" she whispered. "She's talking to him!"

"What's she saying?" squeaked Francine.

"How do I know! Wait a minute." Skip dared another glimpse and this time she groaned aloud. Angela was pointing at her own house.

Jean pushed her aside. "Here. Let me look. Hey, what's she telling him?" Jean ducked down. "He's looking over here," she hissed. "If she tells on us, I'll . . ." She grabbed Skip's arm, "She can't tell anything, right? What does she know?"

Skip couldn't answer that. How much Angela understood wasn't always clear. Maybe she was telling on them but then again maybe she didn't know what was going on.

She dared to poke her head out again. Relief flooded her. Kaminsky and Angela were in the rose garden. He was showing her the flowers. It was okay. They were safe.

It was that evening when the blow fell.

Skip was in her room fixing the scrapbook her sister had messed up when her father called to her.

She heard a stranger's voice as she walked down the hall to the living room and there was Kaminsky sitting on her father's favorite chair. Angela sat on the footstool before him, spreading her velvets on his knee. Her mother and father sat together on the couch.

When Skip appeared her father said, "Well, here she is. My daughter Skip. Say hello to Mr. Kaminsky, honey." He patted the sofa. "Come sit by me."

The sudden lightheadedness she felt when she saw Kaminsky sitting with her family left her. Her father wasn't angry with her, so he didn't know. She sat down and nestled in the crook of her father's arm.

Kaminsky gathered up Angela's many-colored velvet pieces and handed them back to her. "Very nice," he said, but there was no warmth to his smile. He had put on a clean shirt for the occasion, but his frizzy hair stood up in spikes around his bald spot. He reached into his pocket and took out a safety pin.

Skip stiffened.

He held it out to Mrs. Berman. "Angela here told me this belongs to you."

Skip's mother took it and turned it around in her hand. She said in a puzzled way, "Well, I don't know what to say. All safety pins look alike, but if she said, she must have had a reason. What about it? What's it got to do with my Angela?"

"Nothing with her." Kaminsky edged to the rim of his chair and said to them earnestly. "Now look, good people, what I got to say might be foolishness to you, but not to me. You sit here safe in your chairs hearing an old man complain about a safety pin. Crazy, eh?"

Her father said warily, "Not at all, Kaminsky. What's on your mind?"

"This same pin was stuck in my doorbell this afternoon. Like that other night, Berman? You remember? The same thing happened? Also another time before that. Eh! Such foolishness. I didn't bother to tell you."

"Sure I remember! And now again. You shouldn't be pestered like that. Angela, tell Daddy, why did you tell Kaminsky this pin belongs to your mother?"

"Her dress was falling down." Angela threw back her head, to laugh at such a funny thing.

Now it dawned on Mrs. Berman. She turned to Skip to say sternly, "That friend of yours, Jean somebody. I gave her a safety pin for her hem. Were you a party to this? I want the truth, young lady. Did she use it to pester Mr. Kaminsky? Did she push it in his doorbell?"

"No, Mama. She didn't," said Skip faintly.

Her father stirred impatiently, "Skip wouldn't be involved in such a fool thing!" he told his wife. "Besides, I told her to try to find out about this. I know she'd tell me if she knew anything. Right, honeybunch?"

Skip, who was deep in the crook of his arm, moaned to herself. She felt the warmth of his skin through his shirt and smelled his beloved father odor and felt like a traitor. He trusted her. But whose trust was more important—his or her best friend's? When she was with him, like now, his was. But when she thought of telling on Jean she couldn't stand it.

While she was wrestling with this, everyone else was looking at Angela. Mr. Berman was about to question Angela again when his wife put a restraining hand on his arm. She was the one who would ask.

She said to Angela, "Tell Mama, did that girl take the pin I gave her to play with this man's doorbell? You know what I'm talking about, sweetheart? The safety pin for the girl's dress? You remember," she urged.

Angela opened her pure blue eyes wide. "No, Mama, no." She continued to shake her head at her mother to be sure she knew the answer to that one.

Mrs. Berman was satisfied. Her Angela couldn't lie. She held her palms out to Kaminsky to show him they had proved their case. "Sorry, Mr. Kaminsky, we can't help you. Safety pins aren't exactly rare, are they? Maybe you should ask some of the other parents in the neighborhood. There are some rotten apples on every block. On the other hand, kids will be kids. Thank God, no harm done."

Kaminsky raised his shaggy head to look at her straight, his expression unreadable. "No, no harm."

She raised herself from the couch briskly. "Now, can I offer you a cup of coffee? Girls, bedtime. Say goodnight to Mr. Kaminsky. I'll be in in a little while, Angela."

Skip was only too ready to leave this scene. She jumped up.

Kaminsky lumbered to his feet also. He ran his palm over his bald spot, raising higher his halo of hair. He shook his shaggy head. "No coffee for me, Missus. Keeps me awake like my eyes are stuck open. I already got troubles sleeping at night. In my chair I sleep, in my bed, no. Well, what can you do? Many thanks to you anyhow. I'm sorry to disturb you for nothing. Angela, come see me, we'll talk roses."

"I'll see you to the door," said Max Berman. "I think the whole thing is a damn shame. We'll get to the bottom of this. So senseless. For what reason I'd like to know?"

"Ah Berman, you don't need sense for cruelty. Maybe you need anger more. Reasons go deep. Sometimes not even the bad apple like your wife says, not even he knows. He just does, he or she, no thinking to it. Like an animal. He's got an itch so he scratches with what's handy. Feelings don't matter, especially other people's. Excuse me for the lecture."

Skip knew he was wrong. Jean Persico wasn't like that. It was just that . . . Her father drew her closer as he stood at the door with Kaminsky. Safe in the circle of her father's arm, she smiled as she was taught and said good-bye nicely.

She saw how Kaminsky tried to smile but couldn't. Cruel, he had said. Like an animal, he had said. She dimly sensed that that was part of Jean Persico's power. She didn't care about feelings or laws or being good so far as Skip could tell. She wasn't like the rest. She was untamed. Wonderful.

ELEVEN

The next afternoon, Mrs. Berman was at Kaminsky's front door with Angela.

"Oh, did we wake you up? I'm so sorry," she said when Kaminsky opened the door. His face was more creased than usual and he still looked half-asleep. He had dozed off in his chair after lunch while looking at some old snapshots. Her ring had startled him awake, spilling the photos from his lap to the floor.

"No, no," he protested, "It's all right. An old man drops off when he shouldn't. Well, well, who have we here? Don't tell me, let me guess. I think it's my friend Angela from across the street. Am I right?"

"You're right!" Angela squealed, overjoyed. Kaminsky guessed right. She showed him her cigar box. "I have my buttons in here," she told him.

Her mother and Kaminsky began to say something at the same time. They stopped short and smiled awkwardly at one another.

"First you," he said with an old-fashioned bow of his head.

"I was going to say that Angela pestered me all morning, she was that anxious to visit. You did say she should come see you. Remember? Last night? You have to be careful when you say that to her. You have to mean it." Mrs. Berman lifted her eyes from her daughter to Kaminsky. "She's a very loving child," she said simply.

"I know that," he told her, nodding his heavy head. "What I was going to tell you was that you named her one hundred percent correct. Look at her in her white dress and that hair. She's as pretty as an angel, your Angela."

If he had handed Mrs. Berman a crown of gold she couldn't have been more pleased. Whatever she had held against him at first meeting had disappeared.

"Yes," she sighed. Then in a burst of friendliness she said, "You know, she'll be starting school here in a week or so, right after Labor Day. There is a school near the Concourse, for people with . . . for children like Angela. The Kingsbrook School, it's called. She'll be going there." She straightened Angela's dress with a practiced hand, just to touch her child.

"'Zat so?" said Kaminsky. "Very nice. And what will they teach her there?" He regarded Angela's mother with curiosity.

Angela had the answer. "A job!" she told him triumphantly. "They teach me and I g-g-go do it. Mama said."

Mrs. Berman listened to her daughter with an encouraging smile on her worn face. Kaminsky understood that hopeful look. A mixture of irritation and sorrow flushed through him. He thought to himself, Ach, she thinks of miracles that one, a screw missing, like her child. In this world what's to hope for? She'll learn.

He said aloud, "Good. A job. And now Miss Angela, you'd like maybe to come inside? Come. We'll find something to do."

"Flowers," said Angela firmly, looking at his jaunty roses in the garden at their side.

He nodded and poked his head past his visitors to look up at the sky. Overhead was a solid block of gray. A slight wind sprang up, skittering the trash along the curb. There was a rising smell of dampness and dirt that Kaminsky sniffed at like a weatherman.

He said, "Hmmm. Looks like rain. Good. A relief from the heat plus good for my roses. You want to see flowers, we'll maybe visit the family on the wall if it rains. Well, my doorstep is no place to talk. Come. Come in." He added out of politeness, "You too, Mrs. Berman."

"Thank you, but if you're sure it's all right, I'll just leave her here. I've got so much to do. My other girl, well she disappeared after lunch and she usually keeps an eye on her. I don't know what comes over young people today, do you, Mr. Kaminsky? I used to be able to depend on that one. Now, every time I turn around she has disappeared. My Angela now, she likes to be helpful. Always. She's so good in the house. But I'm wallpapering this afternoon and she gets the paste all over herself. It's so hard . . ."

Mrs. Berman must have heard the rising whine in her own voice because she stopped and forced a little laugh. "I talk too much. You can't imagine how much there is to do when you move. Never again. I swear it!"

Angela reproved her. "Don't swear, Mama."

This allowed Kaminsky and Mrs. Berman to share an amused glance. They parted with his promise to bring her straight home if she was a nuisance.

He took Angela through the kitchen to the living room where he went around turning on the table lamps. "It's getting dark in here," he told her.

Angela looked around the small low-ceilinged room as if in a foreign country. People wearing funny clothes sat behind glass frames on the wall. Covering the floor was a threadbare Oriental rug. The walls were papered with long loops of jungley leaves that enclosed the room like a rain forest. A glass-doored china cabinet stood on spindly legs between two windows, home for a few lonely pieces of hand-painted dinnerware. Two maroon easy chairs faced one another on either side of the fireplace. The cushion on one of the chairs sagged deeply. The cushion on the other chair was plump and new looking.

Kaminsky motioned her to the good chair but she didn't want to sit. She put her cigar box on it and knelt on the floor to pick up the photographs Kaminsky had spilled from his lap when he had answered the door.

"That's a good girl. Put them back in that cardboard box."

She fell to studying the photos one by one, bringing them up close as if she were nearsighted. Recognition lit her face at one of them. "A cow!" she declared, holding the snapshot up to Kaminsky who had sat down in his chair.

He took it from her and examined it with an amused grunt. "Jadwiga. A foolish Polish cow. She liked to kick over the pail after I milked her. From my Aunt Julka's farm she was, where I was brought up."

This excited Angela, "Aunt Julka is a rose, a rose on the wall. Here, I'll show you." She pulled on his arm, but he resisted her.

"That's right. Once my aunt, the only mother I knew, now a rose. And here's one with all my cousins, also now roses in my garden."

One by one Angela handed him yellowed photographs and he told her about each one even though her attention wandered. She was mainly interested in putting them neatly back into piles inside the box.

The fact that this didn't mean anything to her made it easy for him to reminisce aloud. He showed her what he had looked like as a tall skinny boy of nineteen with a cap sitting high on his frizzy hair. "That was me just before I left the farm and came here to America." He smiled ruefully at the boy he was. "I was some looker in those days!"

The next snapshot he pored over. He touched it tenderly with a gnarled finger. It showed a glowing young woman in a long skirt with a pile of chestnut hair wound around her head. She was laughing up at the same skinny boy, young Kaminsky.

"Here," he murmured. He passed the photograph back to Angela. "My wife, Sophia. When she was young. Not much older than you are now," he said.

"P-pretty," said Angela smiling at the old photo. She too touched the face in the picture. "Pretty," she repeated.

While her head was bent to it, he tipped his head back and closed his eyes to see the past better. His heavy voice rumbled over her and he spoke as if letting go a secret to an empty room.

"I carried that picture with me when I left the village and six more years until I could send for her. My Sophia. More than forty years in this country and her heart stayed in two places—back home in the village and here in America with me." A groan escaped him and he cried aloud, "Why did I do it! Why?"

Angela looked up at him startled. He took her hand, speaking to her as if to a confessor, "She begged, you see, always begged to go home, home to our village, to Wolska. And over the years we did—to see our families. This last time for her sick mama, we went. To say good-bye, Sophia says to me, and with those eyes, who could resist? So why did I do it? I knew war was coming. But war seemed so far from our village, not even a dot on the map."

He was barely whispering now, his eyes on some inward and tormented vision. "I can see her just as plain as I see you. She had a red kerchief on her hair. 'Bye-bye sweetheart,' I told her, 'I have to leave you now.' My job . . . I had to come home. She wanted to stay. 'Please, Theo, Mama needs me. I must stay just a little longer.' So what could I do? For my lousy job we said good-bye. 'Bye-bye my darling, see you soon, see you soon.'"

Kaminsky dropped Angela's hand and covered his eyes with his fists. "I never saw her again. She got caught. Caught by the war."

Angela kneeled and pulled his balled hands away. "What's the matter?" Why was Kaminisky hiding his eyes?

His sharp blue eyes were filmed and bloodshot, "The matter? The matter is the Nazis with the gas ovens and the big appetite. Hungry for Jews, those ovens, so the Nazis came to Wolska and fed them my family. My Sophia too, I'm sure of it."

Angela knew who Sophia was. She put the snapshot in his hand. "Here she is!" she crowed.

Kaminsky took the picture and whispered to it, "Nu, Sophia, so where are you? You got caught in the war, but the war is over. The camps are empty, the bones cooling off. Are yours there? Those people, the searchers, they mean well, they keep in touch. 'If she's alive we'll find her' they tell me. Keep hoping, they say. Ach, if you should see me now, my Sophia, what I have become. A man without hope is no man."

He tossed the snapshot back in the box. In a sudden angry movement he leaned over the cardboard box and swooped up an armful of old photos, letting them drop helter-skelter. Angela cried aloud and went after them, picking them up where they scattered over the rug.

"Look what you did!" she scolded. "All over the floor."

"Over the floor, on the wall, in the box, what does it matter? You know what a person is without a family, Angela? Look at me, because I'm telling you something you won't hear in school. You know my roses out in the garden?"

He held her chin to face him. Angela nodded. She knew those roses.

"What happens to them if they don't have roots?"

She didn't know the answer to that one but she looked to the ceiling as if concentrating hard.

He said, "Okay, okay. I'll tell you. They dry up like me."

A clap of thunder rattled through the room. The lights dimmed for a moment but didn't go off. Heavy rain pelted down, billowing the curtains, spattering the rug through the open windows.

Kaminsky ran around closing windows in his house. While he was in the back of the house closing his bedroom windows, there came another tremendous thunderclap.

Above the boom he heard Angela's scream. He found her trying to bury her head under the cushion of his chair. She was terrified of the noise. When he pulled her close to him to calm her down she twisted away so she could cover her ears, screaming all the while, "Mama! Mama!"

Kaminsky sat on the floor next to her. He put her head against his chest to say, as quietly as he could, "Sha, sha, it's all right. It's only thunder. It won't hurt you. There's nothing to be afraid of." The soothing words poured from him like syrup. He rocked her like the baby he and Sophia never had.

The rumble of thunder sounded farther and farther away. The storm was moving off. Still, the girl clutched him, although she no longer screamed.

Above her head, Kaminsky caught the sight of the cigar box on the chair. He recalled seeing Angela sitting on her steps, playing contentedly with her buttons.

He managed to hand her the box. "Here, show me what you have here."

The sight of her box did the trick. She was all calmed down. She sat up and lifted the lid.

Angela smiled down at the contents and turned it upside down. A jumble of buttons, spools of thread, pieces of velvet and various kinds of pins spilled out on the rug.

Kaminsky watched her separate the items into piles. He gathered up the safety pins and began to make a chain of them for her amusement. It was in his mind that she would play with it while he telephoned Mrs. Berman. The memories had exhausted him. He had had enough for one day.

Then he remembered the safety pin he had found in his doorbell. He held one up to her. "Angela, did you see who put this in my doorbell?"

"Sure," she said. "I w-wanted to go too. See the flowers."

"Who was it?"

"Somebody. I don't know." She picked up a piece of velvet and stroked it.

"Was it Jean Persico? Your sister's friend Jean, the big girl?"

"Oh no," said Angela. She picked up a straight pin. "She used this one. She s-s-said." She put her hands over her ears. "It rang and rang."

"Wait a minute." Kaminsky was confused. He held up the straight pin. "She was the one who used this the night you were here with your Daddy, correct?"

"Yes. I heard her. It was f-f-fun, she said."

"But some other girl did the same thing yesterday. Right? Not Jean."

Angela laughed at him. "It's a joke on Mama. She gave the p-p-pin for the dress. Jean didn't want it. She g-g-gave it to that girl. I wanted to g-go with her. See the flowers."

Kaminsky understood now. He knew who the culprit was. He'd see to it that he wasn't bothered anymore. Her brothers, those men from the garage, they wouldn't allow this. Them he would tell.

TWELVE

The storm had broken the heat wave. When Skip awoke the next morning, the day was fine. The sun was out and her room had cooled off.

It all made her heart sink.

She absently pulled on her shorts and top, saying to herself over and over, why couldn't it rain, why couldn't it rain? It would have been an excuse. She could have said to Jean, "My mother won't let me go out in the rain."

That sounded pretty lame even to her ears. No, she'd have to go through with it. It was her turn to be initiated into the club. Jean the genius had done it again. She had thought up a dare for Skip that was too scary for her. And pretty soon she was going to be doing it.

Plenty of kids steal, she told herself. They do it all the time. So why was it so hard for her?

"Do you need anything from the Five-and-Ten?" she asked her mother at breakfast. Since she was going to have to steal from it, it might be safer if she did actually buy something.

Her mother didn't need a thing. "Why?" she asked. "What are you doing in Woolworth's?"

"Oh nothing. We're just walking to the Avenue, me and my friends. I just thought you might want something." She bent over her cornflakes, her hair falling over her face. Mrs. Berman was holding Angela's milk glass for her again. It was a sight Skip wasn't up to this morning.

Her mother said, "Well, that's thoughtful, I must say. I tell you what. You take your sister along so she can buy some buttons." To Angela she said, "Would you like that, sweetheart?"

Angela nodded eagerly, which jiggled the milk glass. Two white streams ran down the sides of her mouth.

As usual, the automatic protest rose to Skip's throat, but a flash of sense made her hold her tongue. What she realized in that instant was that maybe having Angela tag along would give her the excuse she wanted more than her next breath. She would tell Jean she had to take care of her sister today and Jean would understand and say well, that's too bad, you can't do it if she's along, I'll just think of something else for you.

Skip said, "Okay, Mom," and slid off her chair more hopeful than when she sat down. "You get ready, Angie."

Her mother had a look of approval for that and then said, "You're pale this morning. Your color isn't good. Do you feel all right?"

Skip hooked her hair behind an ear and tried a smile, hoping it would improve her looks. "I'm fine, Ma."

As Mrs. Berman carried dishes to the sink and busied herself there, she chatted away. "Well, a walk might do you good. That Jean seems to be a nice girl, though I must say she could use some cleaning up. Mr. Kaminsky was full of suspicions that other night, wasn't he? He was ready to accuse her of tampering with his doorbell. But Angela cleared that up for him, didn't you, my love?"

Skip was stung. "I did too, Mom!"

"Yes, well, of course. I would expect you to. Come along, Angela. You're going out with your friends this morning."

It was one of those perfect summer days when the air is so clear everything shines. The sun warms you and the shade cools you off. As soon as the sisters stepped out of the house their eyes crinkled against the glare. Skip had to shade hers with a hand to see across the street to where her friends waited for her.

The street was full of noise and action. Right in front of their house the red-headed twins were trying to trip up the skaters, putting out a toe as they rolled by. Skip hardly noticed. She had no eyes or thoughts for anything but what lay ahead. She recalled hearing of some kid in her old neighborhood who was caught stealing and the family had to move away.

When she and her sister were halfway across the street, Jean called out loudly, "What is she doing here?" meaning Angela. Francine and Norma were on the top step of the porch playing jacks on the wooden boards. Ellie wasn't there.

When they reached the curb Skip said, "I couldn't help it. My mother said I had to take her today. So . . ." She shrugged to mean what could I do?

"Some other time, okay? For the dare? I can't with her along."

By the time she had finished saying this, Jean was skipping down the steps and the other girls had packed up the jacks game.

Jean brushed her hope away with a laugh. "Are you kidding? This is going to be great! Nothing doing. She'll wait outside with us. Hey, you want to quit, just say so."

Be left out of the club? That was the last thing in the world Skip wanted. The next to the last thing in the world she wanted was to have to steal things from the Five-and-Ten. She would get caught, she knew it. She always did. Even when she passed a note in class the teacher caught her. She was no good at stuff like that.

Jean was wearing a red halter above her navy shorts that left a gap of olive skin. The halter seemed to be a hand-me-down from someone much larger. Jean didn't begin to fill it out, but on her it didn't matter. She was able to carry it off with a kind of unconscious assurance.

Skip recognized the thin chain around her neck that dipped into the halter. It was her locket at the end of that chain. No one could see it but it was hers and the thought gave her a kind of thrill. It was there, down between the breasts, next to the skin. Her face, herself.

She fastened her brown eyes on her friend. She couldn't help it. The air seemed to vibrate around Jean. She was all movement and flash, sucking up whatever attention there was around her like some kind of vacuum cleaner.

Jean was drawn to the gleam of the gold chain around Angela's neck and went right to it. She lifted it with two fingers to examine it. Her arm was dusky against the fair skin.

Angela bent her smooth head, to see her chain in Jean's hand. That hand was as interesting to her as the whole person. She regarded Jean without judgment, the way a child looks with equal interest at a nose or a tree.

Jean said, "Hey, nice. But mine is nicer." She reached down and pulled out Skip's locket, letting it swing in front of Angela's eyes, with a teasing glance at Skip.

"M-my sister has a locket," Angela began.

"Never mind," said Skip.

"Okay," said Jean dropping the chain, grinning at Skip. "Well come on, let's go. It's dare time, everybody!"

"Where's Ellie?" Skip wanted to know. Somehow she didn't want to do this without her. She felt she was being pulled along against her will, the same feeling as when she played tug-of-war with a rope and was being dragged to the other side no matter how hard she tried to dig her toes in and hold back. Ellie would know how she felt.

"She's sick again," said Norma. "I called for her and her mother won't let her out."

Francine pushed out her lips to show doubt. "Hey, if she wanted she could get out of that! We're not going to wait for her."

Skip saw that it was no use. She had never stolen anything from a store before, but that was her dare and she had to do it.

Jean linked arms with hers while Angela held on to Skip's other hand. Francine and Norma followed along. They were headed for the busy Avenue, four long blocks away, where all the stores were.

The side streets they walked on were almost empty compared to the long broad Avenue, their destination. It was lined with one small business after another, an endless succession of stores—hardware, clothing, paints, pickles, bicycles, delis—everything needed from birth to death in the way of service and supplies.

The Five-and-Ten was one of the largest, most popular stores on the Avenue. A few shoppers going in and out of the revolving door bustled past the knot of girls by the display windows where Skip was being given her last-minute instructions.

Norma was hopping with excitement. "Remember, we said three things. It doesn't matter what but it has to be three, isn't that right, Jean?"

Francine had her hand up as if in school. "No, wait, wait! Listen to me. I got a better idea. How about three *red* things? I mean, otherwise it's too easy, Jean. How about Skip has to swipe three red things, no matter what?"

Jean narrowed her eyes on the store windows and considered Francine's idea. She was the calmest one there except for Angela, who was in the circle of girls but looking away, smiling gently at the passers-by. She had no idea what was going on.

"Okay," Jean finally said. She clapped a hand on Francine's shoulder. "Nice idea."

Francine bent her head and grinned at the sidewalk as if she had just won something large.

"Now here's the thing," said Jean. "We hereby dare you to steal three things and if they're not red, they don't count and you're not in the club. You got pockets?"

Skip stuck her hands in her shorts wordlessly to show that she did. Her mouth had suddenly gone dry and she couldn't say a word, could hardly swallow. She started toward the store.

"Hey, Angela, come back. You stay here with us!"

Angela paid no more attention to Jean than if she were the wind. Her beloved sister was going into the store, so she would too.

Skip faced Woolworth's the way the doomed face a firing squad. In a dream of fright she walked blindly into the store. A kind of mist had descended over her eyes. All she heard was the pounding of her own blood in her ears. She had no idea her sister was right behind her.

It was midmorning. The store wasn't crowded. Skip wished there were hordes of people in there. Preferably everyone on earth.

She began walking along an aisle, which one she couldn't say because it was just a blur. Her sneakers seemed to be pounding the wooden floor. "Look at her, look at her!" said the noise. She had to decide what to take but she couldn't seem to focus properly. Calm down, she told herself. Nobody was watching, she said to herself, but didn't believe it for a minute. How did robbers do it, she wondered? How could they stand being so scared and nervous?

Along the side wall toward the back of the store were the fish tanks. Opposite them was the stationery counter, and there she stopped. Her eye was caught by the cover of a small address book. It was red. It could easily fit into the palm of her hand. She didn't want an address book. She didn't need one. She wondered if it could really be called stealing if you didn't want what you took.

The saleslady was busy with a customer. Two other ladies were at the counter talking to one another and not looking. Skip reached out and picked up the little book. Her sweaty hand had it almost at her pocket when she heard someone say loudly, "You there, Miss!"

It was too late to drop it back on the counter so she whipped the guilty hand behind her. As she looked around wildly for the man who caught her she backed against the fish tanks. She dropped the address book inside the bowl with the fish to get rid of it. Her hand was so hot and sweaty she wouldn't have been surprised if the water had boiled.

Again she heard the voice say, "You're not to do that!" She whipped her head around. The saleslady and her customer were looking at something elsewhere and so were the other ladies. Their attention was on another part of the store. Something was going on there but at that moment Skip was too busy dealing with a severe case of relief to care.

It wasn't her they were after! Skip wiped her hands on the seat of her shorts and leaned back against the counter because her legs were spaghetti.

She stole a glance at the fish tank, now the owner of the red address book. It had fallen to the gravel on the bottom with the covers spread so that it formed a tunnel. She watched two goldfish swim through it as if it were a reef from their tropical sea.

The sight of the little book made her realize she couldn't go through that again. She wasn't good enough for crime. How was she going to face the girls if she was such a coward? She'd be out of the club and Jean would be through with her and she couldn't bear it.

For one anguished second she seriously thought of staying in the Five-and-Ten forever. She wouldn't have to face what was outside. She pictured herself as a bent-over old lady wandering up and down the aisles, covered with cobwebs.

A familiar cry resounded through the store. It was her sister's voice! Angela!

She ran to it. A man in a white shirt and black bow tie was trying to pull a card of buttons away from her sister who wasn't letting go. Two sales-ladies were standing by, tut-tutting indignantly but staying clear of Angela's thrashing arms and legs. Some curious customers looked on.

Skip pulled at the man's arm. "What's the matter? Leave her alone! Angie, shut up!"

The manager of the store let go of the button card. "Don't let her get away," he said to the salespeople. To Skip he said, "You know this girl?"

"She's my sister."

"She was caught shoplifting." He took off his glasses and wiped his face with a handkerchief. He dabbed at his neat mustache. His tie was crooked. "She had those buttons in her pocket. Mrs. Bugle here spotted her."

"Yes indeedy," said Mrs. Bugle, shaking her finger at Angela. "She paid no attention to me at all when I asked for the money. Shame on you, girl." She looked around the gathered group for approval. No one gets away with anything when she was on the job, no siree.

Angela clutched Skip's arm crying loudly. Skip took the button card from her and handed it to the store manager.

"All right, all right, stop crying. These aren't your buttons, so what's the big idea?"

"Mama said, Mama said," cried out Angela, who looked for all the world like any ordinary pretty young girl.

The store manager now regarded her with a clear question mark on his long bony face.

Skip said, "My sister wouldn't steal anything on purpose." She was able to look the man in the eye. "In our family we wouldn't do such a thing!"

He turned to her and said lamely, "We turn people in for shoplifting." Once again he stared at Angela, who was giving devoted attention to the button card. "Is she. . . ? I mean, is she. . . ?

"Yeah," said Skip. She dug into her pocket. "I have the money for those buttons. My sister didn't understand."

When the buttons were paid for and everything quieted down, Angela wanted only to be with Skip. She pleaded to go home. She had her buttons, she had what she wanted.

Skip did not. She was beside herself with fury. As she scanned the counters she mumbled wildly under her breath, "Why do I have to have her with me! Why couldn't she stay outside? What'll I do now! I can't with her! I'll never be able to . . ."

Close to the entrance, they stopped at the cosmetics and jewelry counter. Skip turned away from it to see if she could spot her friends outside the big glass window. There they were, waiting for her and her pockets were empty. It was hopeless and her life was ruined. Her sister had ruined it. There was Norma looking at her, spreading her hands, asking in dumb show what was going on. Skip shrugged.

Meanwhile Angela was making glad little cries over a string of blue beads. She placed it around her neck and went over to the mirror at the end of the counter to admire herself. The saleslady, who had been party to the fuss over the buttons, kept a suspicious eye on her.

Angela pulled at the beads so the clasp wouldn't show. The string broke. Blue beads went bouncing along the wooden floor every which way. She threw herself to her knees and began to pick them up. So did the saleslady of that counter. Other salespeople from other counters came over to join in the hunt for the beads.

Skip turned to the counter and saw only backs of people bent over the floor. Not a soul was looking at her.

As if she were rummaging in her own dresser drawer, she calmly and deliberately chose red earrings, a red comb and a lipstick in a red case. These she stuffed into her pocket.

She pulled Angela up from the floor. The saleslady lifted her head to yelp, "Get her out of here!"

"Oh, I will," said Skip, and grasping her sister's hand in wonder and gratitude, she did.

THIRTEEN

Skip floated out of Woolworth's and over to her waiting friends on a wave of astonished triumph. It was done. It was done and over with and she hadn't been caught.

"Let's get out of here!" she said to them. Away, away from the store was her first need.

She was so quick to sprint away that she bumped into a delivery boy carrying a stack of cardboard boxes piled to his nose. They tumbled out of his hands like a waterfall of blocks. His pimpled face flushed with outrage but Skip, still so lighthearted with relief, shot him a look of such apology and glee that his anger had no place to go. Her feet said *move*, but she couldn't leave him with boxes on the ground. She helped him stack up the boxes again, bubbling with nervous laughter. By the time that was done, the other girls had run past her and were out of sight. Only Angela remained.

The Avenue was rowdy with noisy strangers hurrying by but so far no one had come shouting out of the store accusing her of shoplifting.

She took her sister's hand and ran with her until

they turned the corner. It was like turning off the radio, the quiet was so sudden.

Jean Persico, Francine and Norma were there waiting for her, leaning against the brick of the closest apartment house.

When Skip ran up to them they gathered around her.

"Okay, let's see!" said Jean, exhilarated by the morning's episode.

Little Norma looked at Skip with her soft licorice eyes openly admiring. She told her that she never would have had the nerve to do what she just did.

Francine had her eyes greedily fixed on Skip's pockets. Her mouth was open as if expecting cream puffs.

All this attention felt pretty good. Skip pulled the booty from her pocket one at a time. "Red earrings, red comb, red lipstick. That was my dare and I did it."

Angela was tall enough to see over Norma's head. "Ooh, Mama will like what you bought." She took her card of buttons from the paper bag. "See what I got?" she said to the backs of their heads.

Skip gazed at the objects in her hand and suddenly couldn't wait to get rid of them. She couldn't stand them. She didn't want to have anything to do with them.

She held up the earrings to Jean. "Here. You want these?"

"Hey, thanks!" Jean removed them from the white square of cardboard and put them on. The shiny hoops dangled past her cheek almost to her neck.

"Gorgeous," breathed Francine lifting one on a finger. "You could be a singer in a nightclub with these."

Angela was open-mouthed at such glamour, but also puzzled. "Where's Mama's earrings?"

Skip said sharply, "You just forget about it, understand Angie? Mind your own business. Go on, walk on up ahead. I'll catch up."

"Yeah, go on," said Jean with such force that Angela took a few steps away. Then she came back.

Skip held the comb up to Francine. "Here. You want this?"

"Well, as long as you're giving things away, I'll take the lipstick, okay? I mean, if it's all the same to you."

Norma put in quickly, "I can use the comb. My mother wouldn't let me have lipstick anyway."

All the way home, Skip was aware of Jean's approving arm around her shoulder. Jean had just told her she was her best friend again. That was worth stealing for.

She and Jean walked the four long blocks, a shady canyon of tall apartment houses, without exchanging a word. Skip was in a dream. Her own family had disappeared somehow and there she was, an orphan, and she and Jean lived together and were sisters. What would it be like, she wondered, to have a sister you weren't ashamed of, a sister you loved.

They finally reached their own corner and turned right at LoPatti's drugstore. Skip, back in her neighborhood of higgledy-piggledy houses and darting children, felt as if she had returned to her own small town after a hazardous visit to the big city.

They all agreed to meet at the clubroom that afternoon.

"Ellie's turn next," said Jean. "Anyone know what she hates most? Snakes maybe?"

Her eyes fell on Kaminsky's garden down the block. The blooms were about at their peak. The clarity of the air along with brightness of the day made their colors stand out like flags. It was as if the sun were shining from inside each petal.

"Maybe she can give Kaminsky another present."

Angela heard this with pleasure. "A p-present." She nodded her head and cried out his name with the joy of recognition.

"What about yours?" asked Norma boldly. Skip noticed that Norma could get away with saying things like that to Jean.

Jean thought this was funny. "Mine? You mean my dare? Sure. You guys want to think up something for me? Go ahead. Maybe I'll do it and maybe I won't." She dared them with bold eyes.

They all laughed at this as if it were a big joke. But Skip knew it was true. Whatever Jean wanted she could do. Nobody, nobody would stop her or even want to. As if she had spoken this aloud, Jean flashed a knowing smile at Skip that said yes, you and me. Whatever that smile promised, Skip wanted.

She floated home for lunch. As she turned the knob on the door to their house, Angela called out across the street to Kaminsky in his garden.

He waved and said, "Wait please. One moment."

He pulled off his work gloves and crossed the street to them. It was a cool enough day for him to be wearing a blue work shirt, soft as a hanky from many washings and threadbare around the collar. Over it were the black suspenders.

His face creased in a smile at the two girls and his eyes, made bluer by the shirt, were lively. "I'd like to speak with the Missus. Your mama. Be a good girl, Angela, and tell her Kaminsky is here."

While Angela was fetching her mother, Kaminsky and Skip smiled uncomfortably at one another. He tilted his head and examined her face as he would one of his flowers. "You know something? I see a resemblance. Yes. You and your pretty sister. Not the coloring, but definite."

Mrs. Berman came to the door before she had a chance to tell him she was nothing like Angela. Nothing.

Her mother said to him, "How are you, Mr. Kaminsky? I thank you again for looking after Angela yesterday. Such a storm! You want to speak to me?"

He waved away her thanks. "Yes. An invitation." He gestured at the riotous flowers in his garden and like a man in love, said, "My roses. I invite you to see them." He raised an index finger for her to mark his words. "Never has there been such a year for my roses. I pick them day after tomorrow so now is your chance. Sunday afternoon starts the flower show at the Temple and this year Kaminsky will win. Guaranteed." He was trying without success to hide how much this meant to him.

Mrs. Berman said, "Well thank you for the invitation. I do believe I will step over this afternoon, but not now. It's lunchtime," she reminded him. "I have some hungry girls to feed."

"Of course, of course. You come. I'll be there. I'll show you something you don't see every day."

He was about to turn away when something occurred to him. "Oh, by the way, tell your husband I found out who was playing such tricks on an old man. You remember my trouble with the doorbell? Your Angela here told me who did it. So tell him that the mystery is solved."

Skip stiffened by her mother's side and regarded the old man with wide eyes.

"Oh?" said Mrs. Berman, "Angela told you? And who was it may I ask?"

Kaminsky thumbed to a house across the street. "It was that rotten kid from over there. Jean Persico. She's the one."

"Skip's friend?" Mrs. Berman glanced down at her stricken daughter and then back at Kaminsky. "You're sure?"

"Sure I'm sure. Otherwise I don't accuse. Like you said yourself, Angela doesn't lie. We just didn't ask her the right question."

"No, she doesn't lie. She doesn't know how. Amy Louise, did you know about this?" Only when her mother was truly angry would she call Skip by her real name. "Never mind, I'll tend to you later. Mr. Kaminsky, what are you going to do about it?"

"Me? Nothing. I wouldn't lower myself. I'll tell her brothers when they get home tonight and let them take care of her." He raised two fingers to his forehead in a farewell salute. "Good-bye for now."

Skip flew to her room and closed the door. She leaned against it, wishing it had a lock. Wildly, she thought of pushing her bed and dresser against it like in the movies. What she wanted most of all was not to face what was coming.

She heard her mother's footsteps coming down the hall. The knob turned but Skip blocked the door with her body.

Her mother knocked sharply. "Let me in, I want to talk to you."

Skip wasn't ready to let her in. She had to think what to do, what to say. "I don't feel so good, Mama."

Her mother knocked again. "I bet you don't. If you don't let me in this minute, you can stay there all afternoon. When your father comes home tonight you can explain yourself to him."

After a few quiet seconds her mother gave up. She went back to the kitchen to give Angela her lunch.

Skip threw herself on the bed. What a tangle she was in, she thought, and all so dumb. Over a little doorbell, a nothing. Betrayed by her own sister, the traitor.

What occurred to Skip at that moment was that she would lose Jean. She might never speak to her again when she heard that Skip's sister told on her. The current between them this morning, the special favor she was in, that wouldn't matter. Jean was like that. She didn't care, didn't care what she did to people and that was part of why she was so exciting.

Skip reached for her pillow and tucked it under her head. Her eyes closed and an image drifted into her mind.

She saw herself as part of a wolf pack running wild in the hills. Jean Persico was the leader, the head of the pack, howling them on. Skip ran after her, untamed and free. No family, no rules, no shouldn't s, no caring, no limits. She was shed of all that and good riddance. It was wonderful.

Then the picture shifted and suddenly the head wolf turned on her for no reason, snarling and snapping at her, forcing her to leave the pack.

Her eyes sprang open. The thought brought her feet from the bed to the floor. She wandered aimlessly about her room, biting her thumb to help her think. She reviewed in her mind how Angela could possibly have known about Jean sticking the pin in Kaminsky's doorbell.

Bits of conversation came back to her. They were all on her steps after Norma's tree dare. She recalled Jean telling Norma how easy it was to keep a doorbell ringing. She had told her that when she did it the other night she had used a straight pin.

Angela was there and listening. It didn't seem possible that she would understand what Jean was saying, or connect it with Kaminsky, but then, you never knew with Angela. Skip had learned that you couldn't predict how much she understood. Sometimes it was more than you thought, sometimes less. That's how she knew. Jean had told her herself.

She leaned her elbows on her dresser top to stare at her reflection in the oval mirror above it. She didn't see her wide eager eyes or that her chestnut hair held glints of red or that her round cheeks were rowdy with health. She saw only her flaws. Her mouth was too big, her eyebrows too heavy, her nose a disaster.

Kaminsky is crazy, she thought. I don't look anything like my sister. But then, as she gazed at herself in the mirror with that in mind, she caught something . . . she didn't know what. She had never noticed it before. There was a hint, some touch of family resemblance, something Angela-like in the face that stared back at her.

It made her turn away fast. She didn't want that. The thought rose that maybe Kaminsky wouldn't say anything about Angela telling. But Skip knew that Jean Persico would figure out who had blabbed. And then what? What would Jean do?

Again the image of the wolf pack came to mind. Only this time they were in a circle and in the middle was a helpless rabbit with Angela's face.

FOURTEEN

In the cool of the afternoon Kaminsky sprayed his roses and carried on several conversations in his head.

He was on the phone speaking Polish with the lady from the agency. Regular telephone pals they were. Years of talking, a voice without a face. Soon he would go back in the house and call her again. Now he was rehearsing what he would say.

He was fluent and patient. His boyhood language came back to him easily. Not like the last time when the woman on the other end kept saying, "What? What? Say that again." Also not once did he lose his temper. This time she wouldn't hang up on him.

In his mind he smoothly said to her, "Of course I understand it takes time to track down survivors. I have been waiting for the final word about my wife for a long, long time. The others in my family I know about. Aunt Julka, Uncle Stanis, Cousin Lech, my family . . . all gone to the Nazi ovens. Dead I can accept. It's the not knowing that kills me. I tell you the truth, Mrs. Kac, I've given up. My Sophia is dead and gone. It's time I gave the rose her name. Put her up on the wall with the rest. You know it and I know it."

As he said those words in his head, all resolutions of patience left him. Without realizing it he switched to English and began shouting into the phone, "So leave me alone already. You people make me crazy with your leads that lead nowhere. This time you tell me maybe she's the one, I should come look. Not again. No more false alarms, please. It hurts too much. I got my roses. Leave me alone so I can mourn my wife in peace!"

Kaminsky found himself aimlessly holding the hose, making a puddle at the base of his cousin Valeria. He fished a handkerchief out of his pocket to wipe the tears from his face.

Resolutely, he put that conversation out of his head and began another.

He was face to face with the kid's brother, the older one who has the garage. The other, the younger one he had seen only a few times. It was enough to size him up. A lightweight that one, cared only for his fancy clothes, eyes not to trust. Also he didn't even return a hello. No point talking to him.

Kaminsky was calm, fair but forceful, like a judge. In his head he said to Jean Persico's brother, "Your young sister has been pestering me . . ."

He started the conversation over again. "Your sister has been tormenting me." That was the word. "This must stop. A childish trick you say, what's the harm, right? A small thing. But not small to me. Listen, a little bee sting can kill someone already allergic. Jews know what is persecution for no reason, so I'm allergic. She hurts without caring, your sister. A terrible way to be, agreed?"

"Yes, yes," Kaminsky had her brother say. "Thank you for bringing it to my attention. I will tend to her and see that it never happens again."

That conversation ended so well, Kaminsky gave himself over to what he would say at the flower show when they gave him first prize. But first he had a word to say to his roses. In his mind he spoke to them. "Listen, you people, I have tended you with my heart and my fat old body. Aunt Julka, you never looked better, believe me, not even in your Sabbath best. Uncle Josef, you used to moan what a loser you were, and now you're a winner. Cousin Ignatz, little Valeria, listen all of you, to what I'm saying this Sunday when I win for you the prize."

He saw himself in front of the crowd at the flower show and said, "On behalf of my family who lives on for me in these roses, I wish to thank . . ."

Skip couldn't stay closed in her room for another minute. Her legs were on fire to run. She longed to be out on the street where she could run her troubles away, shedding them like clothes.

Not so long ago she was a Daddy's girl, sitting on her steps watching the street with a clear conscience. She was clear as glass then. Anybody could see right through her. Now she was like mud in a jar, and nobody, not even herself, could tell what she was made of.

Also she missed her lunch. Stealing and lying was hungry work. She left her room to go to the kitchen to face her mother. She knew what to say to her now. It was her word against Angela's.

"I'm hungry, Mom. What's to eat?"

Mrs. Berman was doing the washing up and Angela was drying and putting away the lunch dishes.

Skip's mother turned off the water and feigned surprise at seeing her. "Oh? I thought you didn't feel well. All better, are you?"

"Yeah, it was just a bellyache. I'm fine now. Can I have the rest of this peanut butter?"

"There's some bread in the refrig. Finish up that milk too. I have to go food shopping this afternoon. Well, I'm glad the bellyache's gone. When you didn't open your door, I thought maybe it was because . . . Sit down, my girl, I want to talk to you."

Here it comes, thought Skip, sliding into her seat. She concentrated on making her sandwich.

Saved by the bell! Someone was at the front door.

Mrs. Berman said to Angela, "See who that is, sweetie."

"No! I'll go," said Skip already on the run.

She opened the door to Ellie, who grinned at her and said, "Hi. Where's everybody? What did I miss this morning?"

"Ellie!" Skip flung her arms around her. "You're a lifesaver!"

She whispered hotly to her friend, "I have so much to tell you! But I can't now. Get me out of here, will you? We have to find Jean right away. My mother's after me to tell on her about the doorbell. Think of something quick, like I have to go with you someplace, okay?"

As they walked back to the kitchen, Skip squeezed her friend's hand nervously. Ellie was good at making up stories, she knew that from other times. But also it crossed her mind that maybe Ellie was too honest for this. Look at the way she could stand up to Jean when she didn't think something was right. Skip thought to herself, she's so straight I'll never get out of here.

What she didn't know was how many sick afternoons her friend had spent listening to soap operas on the radio. From them she had a store of stories that would shock a warden. All she had to do was choose one. The acting part was easy.

As they entered the kitchen Ellie's lips were parted, panting with urgency. Her eyes were wide, her brow creased. There was a pathetic tremor in her voice.

"Hi, Mrs. Berman. Can Skip come to my house for a while? My mother just had some bad news from her sister in Chicago. You see, the baby needs an operation and my aunt's eyesight is going fast. They have no money because Uncle Jack gambled it away since they let him out of jail."

She stopped to swallow a sob and then bravely continued, "My mom isn't feeling well and wants me to stay with her this afternoon. She said to bring Skip too. It would cheer her up to have her around."

Skip stared at her friend, blind with amazement. She knew she was good, but this was way beyond that.

This deluge of troubles had Mrs. Berman's hand fly to her lips. "How awful! Oh, the poor thing! Your mother must feel just terrible. Of course Skip can go. Go, go."

She went to the counter and handed Ellie a plate with a kitchen cloth covering an inviting shape. "Here," she said. "Take the rest of this angel-food cake to your mother. Fresh baked this morning. Tell her, with my sympathy. Or maybe I should take it over myself?"

"No don't!" cried Ellie, a stricken hand over her heart. "I mean, she's lying down now. She had me put a wet washcloth over her eyes for her headache. Migraine, you know. She always gets those headaches when she hears from my aunt in Chicago. Thanks so much for the cake, Mrs. Berman. Here Skip, you carry it."

She held out a delicate trembling hand for all to see. "I don't trust myself to hold the plate. I get this way when my mother doesn't feel well. Oh, I'm so glad that Skip will be with me!"

Mrs. Berman patted Ellie's hand, touched to the heart.

Angela had listened to Ellie's account with both hands to her cheeks. She was whimpering the way she did at any sadness she saw or heard about: mistreated dogs, injured birds, a sick baby; it all struck her equally to the heart. She needed consoling and turned to her mother for that.

The two girls left with Skip carrying the cake for Mrs. Lefcourt, who was never to see a crumb of it.

As soon as they were out in the street, Skip grabbed Ellie around the waist and danced her up and down, unable to contain her admiration. She couldn't get over Ellie's talent and kept telling her so. "A genius, a genius!" she cried. "And here, I thought you were too honest to do it."

"I'm not, I'm not," said laughing Ellie.

They hurried to the clubroom with the cake. By the time they reached the abandoned house Skip had filled Ellie in on the events of the day starting with the shoplifting and ending with Kaminsky's threat to Jean.

Jean, Francine and Norma were in the clubroom as expected. It was the cake that got the greeting, not them. They fell on it as if they were starving.

Skip had trouble getting Jean's attention for what she had to tell her. Jean had her mouth full while tossing pieces of it at the other girls. White pellets flew around the room.

"A snowball fight," whooped Francine, tossing bits back at Jean.

Finally what Skip was saying began to sink in. It was the words, "your brothers," that stopped the horseplay.

Jean sat down plunk on the arm of her chair. She swallowed hard. "What?" she said incredulously, "Kaminsky is going to tell my brothers? He's going to tell my brothers about me and his stupid doorbell?"

She jumped up and began to walk around aimlessly, her anger filling up the room like bad air. The other girls watched her warily and in silence.

She stopped pacing and glared at them. "How did he find out?" she demanded. "Only you guys knew. Who told?"

Nobody answered.

"Come on, who was it? I'll find out and you'll be sorry."

Skip had to say, "It wasn't us. It was my sister. Angela. She told."

A flick of remembrance passed over her like a dark wave. She was recalling the image she had of Angela surrounded by a pack of wolves. The thought raised the hair on her arms.

Skip pleaded, as much to her conscience as to Jean, "She didn't mean anything by it, you know that. She just doesn't know any better. She was there. You said it in front of her, remember?"

Ellie chimed in. "You can't be mad at somebody like Angela. Can she?" She was appealing to Francine and Norma.

Norma shook her bangs at Ellie and Francine kept her eyes on Jean to see which way the wind was blowing.

Jean had turned her face to the window. She said in a neutral way, "Oh. Angela. I forgot about her. Nah, who's mad?" None of them saw her eyes narrow the way a hungry wolf fixes on his prey before he jumps.

FIFTEEN

Jean persuaded them to walk the eight long blocks to the garage after mulling over Skip's news. She told them that if Kaminsky was going to tell her brothers on her, she would get to them first. Tell it to them her own way. Her girl friends were right there to back her up. Then Kaminsky could complain till he was blue in the face.

"They'll just laugh at him," she told the girls. "He thinks he's going to get me into trouble. He's the one who's in trouble. My brothers will give it to him good."

Skip wanted to see that. She pictured them on white horses defending their sister with drawn swords against Kaminsky. Jean had told her that time in the alley how wonderful they were.

Jean was oddly quiet as she led the way to the garage. That afternoon it was Ellie she favored, walking along with her arm around the girl's waist. There was no way to predict which one of them she would choose as best friend for the day. Skip, who was right behind them, saw Jean's head lean intimately against Ellie's. Brown hair mingled with the red.

Skip followed miserably along. Jean wasn't talking to her. She was mad at her because of what Angela had done. And now she didn't even have Ellie. Norma and Francine were walking hand in hand behind her. They had one another. She was an outcast and had no one.

With self-pity and jealousy burning a hole inside her, she skipped along humming a tune to show them all how carefree she was. The walk seemed endless.

Jean led them where they had never been. They passed along streets as crowded as their own until they crossed the trolley-car tracks. They began to see small factorylike buildings, squat and treeless. Working places instead of private homes. Trucks rumbled along the road as they walked. Tufts of grass grew through cracks in the sidewalk. Skip stepped carefully around the broken glass. She thought how Ellie would make up stories about the empty whiskey bottles.

They turned a corner and Jean stopped. The Persico garage was on a short side street between an unpaved parking lot and an auto supply store at the corner. Across the street from where they stood was the garage. Jean Persico stared at it for a moment and then bent her head to regard the toe of her sneaker. She kicked the pavement with it. Then she picked up a stone from the empty lot behind her and threw it at the lamppost.

Skip noticed that she was in no hurry to cross that street and wondered why.

Norma read the metal sign above the garage aloud. "Ersico Garage. Hey, what happened to the P? It's missing."

Francine glanced quickly at Jean's brooding face and said, "Shut up, Norma."

They waited for Jean's next move.

She finally took a deep breath as if to say, this is it, and crossed the street. The others trailed her like ducklings.

The doors to the garage were open. The only light came through the doorway so that the inside was as dim and clanky as a mine. There was a partially dismantled car with its hood up and its insides on the ground like spilled guts. Nobody was tending to it. Next to it, lifted high in the air by a jack, was another car. An aged mechanic, wearing a baseball cap and oil-streaked coveralls, was banging on its underside.

Jean called out to him, "Hi, Mr. Bergie."

He squinted at the doorway. Jean was just a faceless silhouette against the bright outside light. Mr. Bergie limped over. When he saw who it was, his grimy face cracked open in a wide grin of recognition.

The other girls were bunched behind Jean, peering into the garage with curiosity. Skip drew in the heavy dirty metallic smell and liked it.

Ellie whispered to her, "Where's his teeth?"

"Maybe in the car. You ever see her brothers?" she whispered back.

Ellie shook her head. "Never been in the house," and pinched her. She pinched back. They giggled. Jean reached behind her to punch them quiet. With that exchange, Skip felt risen from the dead. At least Ellie was her friend again.

Mr. Bergie smelled of grease and tobacco. He said,

"Hello yourself. Jean is it? You get so big I don't know you anymore. Tell me. How's the papa?"

"Him? Oh, he's fine."

"Good, good. His boys say he only sits. Well, you tell him I was asking. Tell him Orlando Bergie remembers the old days. Now what can I do for you?"

"Is my brother Manny around?"

Mr. Bergie jerked his head toward the rear of the garage. It was like a dark cave back there. "He's on the phone. You want Paulie, maybe? You go get him at the store. He said he'd be right back half an hour already." He shook his head at the dismantled car. "Manny's gonna bust a gut."

"No, I don't want Paulie. I'll wait for Manny."

"Okay, I'll go see what's doing." He noticed the cluster of girls behind Jean. "Don't come in. Nice girls like you, you'll get yourself dirty."

"That Dodge done yet, Bergie?" Manny Persico strode through the garage toward them. He was a big-shouldered man with a stubble of beard as dark as a pirate's. His beer belly pushed at his coveralls. He looked old enough to be Jean's father. He was wiping his hands on a dirty rag when he saw his sister. "Something wrong with Pop?" he asked anxiously.

"No, nothing like that. Hey, Manny, I walked over 'cause I got something funny to tell you. You got a minute?"

"You come all the way here to tell jokes? I'm busy here. This better be good."

Jean bit her lip and threw a forced smile at her friends before she began. Skip thought she looked scared but then decided it couldn't be.

"You know that old guy Kaminsky, lives two houses down?"

"No."

"The one with the flowers out front."

"Oh him. Yeah?"

"Well, just for fun, just playing around, I stuck a pin in his doorbell. You know, to keep it ringing. Manny, it was so funny the look on his face when nobody was there. You should have seen it!"

Her brother didn't seem to mind missing such a treat. He turned his attention to the stripped car behind him. The sight of it puffed his chest with rage. He bellowed, "Paulie? Where is that goof-off no-good brother of mine. Bergie? This Buick has to go out this afternoon!"

Mr. Bergie said quietly, "He'll be right back, Manny. Keep your shirt on. He had to go get a part next door."

Manny turned back to his sister impatiently.

"So?"

"So nothing. That's it. Just a joke. A stupid doorbell. My friends here can back me up. Just that one time, right, girls?" Now the grin she gave them was blinding in her relief at how easy this was.

They each chimed in with some timid support. So far Jean's brother was not a bit what Skip had expected.

Manny was an overburdened and impatient man. He said to his sister, "Let me get this straight. You came all the way here to tell me this? So now I know. What do you want from me?"

There was more, but now Jean considered herself on safer ground and said more confidently, "Well, he's mad now. Somebody blabbed about me." She threw Skip a look that had a rock in it. "He says he's going to talk to you about it. Probably tonight when you get home. I knew you'd just laugh. Tell him to lay off me, Manny. He's always on my back."

It took a moment for this to sink in. Then, in a swift movement his work-hardened hand lifted and struck Jean across the face.

Skip's mouth opened to gasp in the soiled air without her knowing it.

Manny said to his kid sister, "I run a neighborhood business here! He talks to me, he talks to others. I don't give a damn about Kaminsky or doorbells, but I won't have the name Persico badmouthed around here, you understand that? It's bad for business. Okay you told me. I'll tend to Kaminsky. Now get out of here, go on home."

Jean strode on home ahead of the other girls with her head in the air, not saying a word to any of them. They tagged along in embarrassed silence. They had witnessed the shaming of the unshameable and it was as if the earth had slipped.

Skip sat out on her steps after supper keeping a sharp eye on Jean across the way, who was sitting on her porch steps with her chin resting on her fists. She gave no sign that she knew Skip was there.

The sun still touched the rooftops, but the street itself was shaded and cool enough for an occasional sweater to be draped around a shoulder. After such a comfortable day many families were out in full force on their stoops or porches. There was a good-humored feel to the street this hour, as if there were a truce in the cares of the day.

Every once in a while Jean Persico raised her head to look to the corner of the block. Her brothers were due home.

Kaminsky was out watering his roses in the soft evening air. He too was keeping a lookout for the Persico brothers.

Angela stepped out of the door holding her cigar box. "Mama said I should stay with you," she told her younger sister.

Skip was miserable. She didn't want to look at her. Then she did. There was something she could do that might make it up with Jean.

She said to Angela, "Do you know that you got my friend Jean in trouble? You told on her to Kaminsky! You know what you're going to do? You're going to go over and tell Jean you're sorry. Tell her you didn't mean it."

"Mean what, Skip? Shuh-sure, I'll tell her. What did I do?"

Skip was hustling her across the street. "You told . . . Never mind, just tell her you're sorry, you didn't know it was a secret."

"I duhdidn't know it was a secret," repeated Angela.

When they were at the foot of the porch Jean gave them a hard stare and then turned away.

Skip nudged her sister. "Go on," she said. "Tell her you're sorry."

Before Angela got the words out, Jean said, "Here he comes. G'wan home, get outta here!" It was as if she had never laid eyes on either of them before. She had spotted her brother Manny at the corner grocery. He was on his way home, walking fast, a few houses away.

Kaminsky saw him at that moment also. He turned off his hose to stop him and have his say. They met in front of the Persico house.

The girls had no time to leave. They were there as audience when Kaminsky said to Manny, "Excuse me, Mr. Persico. A word, please?" His big flat face was flushed with all the pent-up words yet to come and his mouth worked as he got ready to say them.

Manny said to him, "Save your breath. I heard already." He lifted his chin toward Jean. "Do yourself a favor, Kaminsky, don't pay so much attention to these kids. You'll live longer." He brushed past the old man, took the steps two at a time and without a nod or hello to his sister, slammed the door behind him.

It had all happened so fast, Kaminsky was left with his mouth open and moving as if still preparing for speech.

He straightened as if his dignity were in his spine. Only then did he notice that he had an audience on the porch steps.

Jean's scornful eyes were on him and the small smile that lifted her lips said louder than words, So there!

Skip, standing at the foot of the steps, bent to tie her shoelace. She was too embarrassed to look at him.

Only Angela had her usual open-mouthed smile for him.

"Hi, Kaminsky. Look, I have my box." She lifted it to show him.

"That's good, Angela. Very good." A smile was beyond him but his big face was gentle as he said to her, "How would you like to come over Sunday morning? Help me pick my roses. You remember? We have to get them ready for the show. You come over, we'll fix them nice."

He was reaching for his good humor, but when he glanced at Jean it failed him. He glared at her and wagged his finger. "I got my eye on you, young lady, and don't you forget it."

"Yah, yah," jeered Jean at his back. He was already walking to his house.

Her eyes followed him as he bent over the flowers in his front yard.

Skip still had her heart set on getting back into Jean's good graces. She said to Jean, who was hugging her knees a few steps above her, "Angela has something to tell you. She wants to tell you she's sorry. She didn't mean it. She didn't know she shouldn't tell Kaminsky." She nudged her sister. "Go on, tell her!"

Jean wasn't interested in hearing whatever Angela had to say. She was watching Kaminsky tend his roses. Her speculative eyes returned to Angela. She stared intently at her as if seeing her for the first time. Then it was back to Kaminsky. Jean was studying them both, biting her thumb, absorbed by some thought. Something was taking shape in her mind.

Suddenly her face and manner changed. Now she

was charged with an idea. The discoverer of fire may have looked the same way.

She rose and jumped down the few steps of her porch to Angela who was shifting from one foot to the other. She was thinking of the words to say, getting ready to speak her piece. Jean picked up Angela's hand and swung it back and forth, grinning at her as if they were best friends. She said to her, "Never mind about telling on me. Forget it. Hey Angela, how would you like to belong to our Dare Club?"

Angela was smiling back, enjoying the movement of her hand in Jean's. She swung the joined hands harder, playing this nice game.

Skip couldn't believe what she had just heard. She cried, "What!"

Jean shone the same smile on Skip who was drawn, ping! the way nails are drawn to a magnet. She had thought she might never receive that smile again and here it was. This time she would never lose it. She would do anything . . .

Jean said to her, "Well sure, why not? It'll be fun for her. We need more members. Go on, go on, tell her about the club. Tell her what fun it is."

Angela knew about clubs from her old school. She had belonged to one that cut out bird pictures from old magazines and had loved it. "You mm-m-mean like in school? We have meetings?" She began to rock on her feet with the joy of it.

Jean said, "Only you have to do something to get in. I'm going to dare you to do something and you have to do it. Then you can belong to the club. Okay?"

"Okay. I c-can do something." Angela rocked back and forth, clutching her box to her breast in ecstasy. "What?" she asked. "What should I do? I'll d-do it."

Jean looked over at Kaminsky's garden once more and said, "I'll think of something nice and easy for you. Let's see. Tomorrow's Saturday. Can you come on over tomorrow night after supper?"

"Can we, Skip?"

Skip was in a whirl with this turn of events. She didn't know what to make of it. Angela in the club? Never! But how nice Jean was. It was heaven. Doubtfully she said, "I guess. I know that Mom said they are going out. I think she said to her high school reunion. So I guess we can. Hey, Jean?"

"What?" She turned a blank stare.

"Oh, nothing, forget it." She wasn't about to oppose Jean now. "Okay, but nothing dangerous. No climbing trees or anything. She can't do that stuff. My mother would kill me."

"Don't you worry. It'll be nice and easy. We'll have fun. You'll see." All the while Jean was absently rubbing the side of her face that had been slapped that afternoon in front of everybody.

SIXTEEN

"Thank heaven for longer dresses," said Mrs. Berman, examining her image in the full-length mirror on her bedroom door. The full black skirt brushed her ankles. "I wouldn't want a single soul of the old crowd to see my legs now," she said to her two solemn girls sitting on the bed, watching her get dressed.

Their mother hiked her skirt up to her knees. "Would you ever know that these sticks were once famous? I was a cheerleader in high school and Tod somebody, tsk! I forget his name, would you believe it? Well he said my legs made the touchdowns, not his. It was in the school paper. Oh yes." She nodded to herself.

Anticipation of the coming evening brightened her deep-set eyes. She had been to the beauty parlor that afternoon and her lavish hair was in a braided crown on top of her head. She was wearing a scooped-neck black silk top tucked into the long black swing skirt. High-heeled platform shoes clapsed about her ankles. Pearls gleamed at her ears and throat.

She twisted to see herself from different angles. "Maybe what this needs is a bright belt. I look like I'm going to a funeral instead of a reunion. Come help me find a belt."

Skip jumped from the bed and ran to the closet where the belts hung from a hook. "Mom?" she said, pausing at the closet door.

"Yes?"

"You look beautiful!"

"Do I?" Her mother said this like a shy child just told something she wanted to believe yet couldn't.

Skip looked at her with big eyes. The way she had said that made Skip feel queer, like being in the room with a stranger. Her mother had always been so sure of everything.

Angela went over to touch her mother's hair and run a soft hand down the rouged cheek. She wanted to touch what her mother wore.

Mrs. Berman stopped her hand and held her daughter's chin to bring her face close to her own. She gazed at the two faces in the mirror, one fresh and vacant, the other worn and knowing, yet the similarity was there. "My other self," she murmured to Angela's image in the glass. And then she said softly, "Forgive me, my darling."

She shook her head at herself and went briskly to her dresser. Rummaging through the top drawer she said, "Now where did I put that snapshot of you in the park last month? I want to show you off."

Skip came to her with a wide red belt. "How about this one, Mom?" Mrs. Berman wrinkled her nose. "Too gaudy," she decided. "Never mind. You go see if your father is out of the bathroom yet. He takes forever to shave. Tell him I'm almost ready and I don't want to be late. Angela and I will find a belt."

Skip's father was patting some lemony after-shave lotion on his cheeks, an odor that she adored. She sat on the rim of the tub and breathed it in. "You're bleeding," she told him.

He lifted his chin and saw the razor nick above the knob in his throat. He tore off a piece of toilet paper and plastered it on the cut. "I think I'll leave it here all night. What do you think?" he asked his daughter. His big, bluff sad-eyed face smiled down at her.

"Mom would love it," she grinned back at him. "She says you should hurry up."

She followed him back to the bedroom.

"What are you girls up to tonight?" he asked, opening a drawer and taking out a white shirt.

"Oh, nothing I guess." Skip thought of the evening ahead and a touch of dread clenched her stomach. She almost didn't want her parents to go. For the millionth time she wondered what Jean was going to dare Angela to do. Why was she being so nice? Nobody in the world would want Angela in the club.

"That's my good girl," her father said absently, absorbed in selecting a tie.

Skip nodded, knowing she wasn't. He didn't know her at all.

Before her parents left there was a list of okays to go through. Okay, we won't stay up late. Okay, I won't leave her alone. Okay, I won't go outside. Okay, we'll have a good time. You too. Okay, don't worry. Skip kept her fingers crossed to undo all the lies.

As soon as her mother and father drove off in the waiting taxi she took Angela by the hand and hurried across the street to Jean's house. Dusk was gathering, but there was enough light left for Norma and Francine to be at their game of jacks on the porch. Ellie was there, looking on.

Jean ran down to them. "What took you so long? I thought maybe you got chicken." Her eyes glistened with excitement.

Angela said, "We did! We got chicken for supper." How did this girl know that?

Suddenly she shivered and looked around mistrustfully at where she was. She pulled at her sister. "Let's go home, Skip." She wasn't used to being out so late.

Jean put her hand on Angela's shoulder and playfully shook it. "Hey, whattaya talking? Don't you remember? It's your big night. You're gonna get into our club."

"Oh yeah! I forgot. I'm g-gonna be in the club."

The other girls had stopped playing jacks and were listening to this. Skip caught the question in Ellie's eye and shrugged to show that she didn't know what to make of this either.

Jean said to Angela, "I told you that I was going to dare you to do something and you have to do it if you want to get in, okay?"

All eagerness, "Okay."

The streetlights weren't on yet but there was an air of closing-down to the street. It was slowly emptying. Voices of mothers calling their children home were a distant song of names. "Jackie, Jackeee?" "Roseaaaanne." "Leeeon, time to come inside."

Lights were on in some homes. Rooms sprang to plain view with windows wide open, the air too delicious this cool August night to draw the curtains.

Jean looked up and down the street in the way spies do when making sure they aren't followed. In a hoarse whisper she said, "I think it's time!"

There was a special stir, a fizz in the air about Jean Persico this night. It drew the girls from the porch to her side. Skip moved closer as if pushed by a hidden hand.

Jean sat Angela down on the bottom step. "Wait here," she said and disappeared inside her house.

"Do any of you know what the dare is?" asked Skip. No one knew.

"What's going on?" asked Ellie. "Your sister is going to be in the club?"

A small ripple of nervous laughter passed through the group and they drew together in a pack. Something was about to happen. They didn't know what, but they sensed it. They wanted it.

Angela sat on the wide wooden step clasping her knees. She smiled up at the girls clumped in front of her, happy to be with them.

Jean returned with a large pair of scissors. She jumped the steps to the bottom and handed them to Angela. She said to her, "To be in our club, this is what you have to do. You see the roses over there?" She waved a hand to the flowering garden two houses away, near enough to be scenting the air.

Angela stood up to see better. "Sure. I s-see the roses. Kaminsky's roses."

"Well, you're gonna do him a big favor. You're gonna cut his roses for him."

A collective sigh went up from the others. For Jean to think of this took their breath away. They shifted their legs and darted glances at one another. Nervous smiles played around their lips.

Jean said to Angela, "But only cut the heads off. You know what I mean? Only the tops of the roses."

Angela stared at the garden. "Cut his roses for him. Only the t-tops," she repeated as if it were a lesson.

She looked down at the scissors she held in her hand and shook her head. She handed them back to Jean, saying, "Kaminsky said I should help him c-cut the flowers. Sunday morning I should come. We're gonna win, he said."

Jean wet her lips and tried again. "So yeah, Kaminsky likes you and you like him, right?" To the other girls she said with a forced laugh, "I'll say. She tells him stories like who put the pin in his doorbell. No wonder he likes her." She hadn't bothered to lower her voice, as if Angela were deaf and couldn't understand. Angela understood the words but not the malice behind them.

Ellie said to her, "So what are you? Getting even?"

Jean hissed at her, "If you don't like it you can go home, get out of the club. Up to you."

Ellie looked away, her lips parted. At that moment the lamppost at the curb switched on, glinting off the braces in her open mouth. Her palm opened and closed, and her lips moved without her knowing it.

It was plain to Skip that Ellie was torn. She saw her friend look quickly at Angela and then at Jean, trying to decide what to do. Angela was a vague white presence looking off to Kaminsky's garden. Jean was a silent shout, glaring at Ellie, waiting for her answer with her hands balled at her hips. She tossed her head and Skip imagined sparks.

"No, no, I was just asking." Ellie couldn't resist her.

"Okay then. And the same goes for the rest of you. You're either with me or out. How about you, Skip? You with us?"

Skip clamped down on her teeth and nodded. She knew what was happening here. Her sister was about to do a really bad thing to the old man and she was going to let her. Her sister was nothing to her and Jean was everything. She protected that thought. As if she were putting a shoulder against a door, no other thought was allowed in. She wouldn't lose Jean no matter what.

Jean Persico spoke to Angela soft as honey. "I said it was a favor. I know he's gonna bring the flowers to some show tomorrow. We're just saving him the trouble. They only judge the heads of the roses. See? We leave a bunch of them on his doorstep and he'll be surprised. He'll be glad. You want to do him a favor? You want to be in our club? Let's go do it!"

That was enough for Angela. She would do Kaminsky a favor.

Jean led the way to the garden and squatted next to it on the path to the house. The other girls did the same. Jean looked up at Kaminsky's house. All the windows were dark except for a dim glow from an inner room that could be seen through the kitchen curtains.

Angela was given the scissors. "Go ahead," she was told, and so she did.

She entered the garden.

Jean whispered, "Here we go." A kind of nasty excitement gripped them all. She had awakened a taste for cruelty.

Skip heard the snip of the first flower head. She saw her sister bend over and cut. She heard the snip of the scissors and then the light sweet voice on the evening air, Snip, "Uncle Josef." Snip, "Cousin Ignatz." Snip, "Auntie Julka." She spoke their names as if greeting people on the street. Snip, snip.

Skip didn't think. She didn't decide anything with her head. It was her body, her gut, her heart, her pumping blood that did the deciding. It made her stand up and cry loudly, "No, Angela! Stop that!"

At that moment a light streamed from the windows of the house. Kaminsky opened his door to see Angela standing there with scissors in hand, the beheaded roses on the ground.

The other girls ran swiftly, melting away unseen. Only Skip stayed frozen in place her mouth still agape with her cry.

Kaminsky was also fixed in his doorway. For a few heartbeats he did nothing but take in the damage to the roses that stood for his lost family. The light from his kitchen bared stems without blooms, necks without heads. Petals were scattered on the ground. Then his head went back and from him rose a high thin suffering sound. It was a cry of loss unchanged down the centuries. It was the age-old cry for the dead. Only for Kaminsky, it was for the twice dead.

At this horrible sound Angela dropped to her knees to put her head down in the dirt and her hands over her ears. She bellowed aloud her fear and Skip was able to go to her.

SEVENTEEN

Angela was put to bed that night, whimpering and feverish, there to stay for several days.

Skip was up and around the next morning, but inside she was a bleeding jumble of confusion and regret. Mostly she stayed in her room wanting only to be with her old friends, the outgrown bears and dolls from long ago. It was as if she had been in an accident and needed time to recover.

She couldn't figure it out. Many times that day she stood by her sister's bed and examined the pale lovely face on the pillow. Rose White her father used to call her, a fairy-tale name. But Angela was real and the same pain in the neck she always was. And when the chips were down, what had Skip done? She had chosen Angela over Jean Persico. There it was; she was connected to her sister in ways she didn't suspect. The weight of family had come down on her, the tie was in her bones and she'd never be free of it.

The one satisfaction she had was that she didn't tell. When her mother and father had returned that night and found Angela in a state, she had only told them that Angela had cut off Kaminsky's roses on a dare. That was all. She wouldn't say who put her up to it.

Her father had demanded the whole truth from her but she was beyond trying only to please him. He knew right away who was to blame, but he wanted to hear it from his once obedient daughter and she wouldn't say. She wouldn't give Jean Persico to him. She was hers.

He was angry and puzzled. His big hands held her shoulders and his dark eyes searched her own as he asked her what had happened to his good girl.

This made her cry out, "I'm not your good girl!" Her arms went up and out to throw off his hands. He didn't know her at all. She hardly knew her own self, so how could he?

That same Sunday afternoon Max Berman crossed the street to ask Kaminsky if he would come see Angela. He described how every once in a while his daughter's face would crumple and she would begin whimpering in this heartbroken way, "Kaminsky's hurt, Kaminsky's hurt." Would he please come over and show the girl that he was okay?

He came. Kaminsky didn't blame Angela for the massacre. "I might as well blame my flowers," he said. He wasn't interested in who was responsible for ruining his roses. It was done. Nothing would bring them back. If he were true to his feelings he would have torn his clothes and worn a black armband. He would be in mourning for the dead.

Instead, he slumped in the doorway of Angela's bedroom and said to her, "Look. Here you see Kaminsky. Don't you worry. I eat, I sleep, so I'm all right. You get better."

He came again on Monday for a few minutes. He repeated what he had said the day before. Angela needed to be convinced all over again. White stubble was beginning to cover his heavy cheeks and chin. He had stopped shaving. His clothes looked like they had been slept in.

Toward the end of that week he stopped at the Berman house carrying a suitcase, there to say goodbye. In the lapel of his jacket was a pink rose. He showed it to Angela who was out of bed, sitting up in her chair. "You see who escaped the scissors? You know her from the picture on the wall? So tell me, sweetheart. Who do we have here?"

Angela glanced at it and turned away.

"No, no, child, don't look like that. Maybe it's a sign, a miracle. You see here the rose with no name. The one I was saving for my Sophia."

He hitched his chair closer to hers. In an undertone he spoke to her like an equal friend. "The agency calls and says this time maybe it's her. My wife. I should come right away. At first I say no, go away, another false alarm I don't need. But now?" He lifted his heavy shoulders in a shrug. "What's to keep me here? It's a chance, a maybe. I thought I had stamped out hope like a bad germ. But then I . . . this rose. It's still alive." He sniffed at it. "Like an old fool I packed my bag. I'm off to the old country on a prayer and a maybe."

He put his big hand to her cheek and said, "Sometimes it's all you get—a maybe. It's enough to give it a try."

Angela smiled her sweet smile at him. Kaminsky was all dressed up and he smelled good again. When he had gone she picked up a piece of her cloth and held it to her face trying to feel again the warm hand.

Earlier that morning Skip was sent to Abchek's grocery store. It was raining slightly, more a drizzle than a full rain but enough to clear the streets. The only people to be seen were the red-headed twins up the block having a puddle fight, seeing who could get the wettest.

As if drawn by a magnet, almost against her will, she crossed the street for a look at Kaminsky's garden. One quick glance was enough. The heads of the roses that Angela had sheared off were still on the ground. Kaminsky hadn't touched them. The rain-soaked petals were strewn about, half-buried in the dirt. The jaunty blooms were no more than litter, no different than the candy wrappers or wads of tissues lying in the gutter. Garbage to be disposed of.

For the first time she was seeing what had been done. A sense of Kaminsky's desolation swept over her. Her sorry face lifted to his door, but she wouldn't have known what to say if he had appeared.

As if waking from a fever, for the first time that week, the thought of losing Jean Persico didn't hurt. All that wet cringy feeling was gone, washed away by a resolve that formed in her mind. Without knowing it, her arms lifted up and out the way they had thrown off her father's grasp. There was one more dare she had to do. The thought of it made her mouth go dry. Skip took a deep breath of damp air and muttered aloud to herself, "Go ahead, I dare you."

It began with walking twenty steps to Jean Persico's house. She counted every one of them. There she stood under her umbella getting up her courage. She rang the doorbell.

Footsteps. Expecting Jean, Skip braced herself as the door opened. It was a man she hadn't seen before. He was dressed as if he were going to a party. She could smell his after-shave lotion and thought he was as handsome as a movie star. His blond hair was in a high pompadour in front, slicked back at the sides. He was putting cufflinks in his ruffled yellow shirt.

He grinned down at her, showing a gap just like Jean's between his front teeth. He must be the other brother, the one that wasn't there the day they went to the garage.

"Yeah?" he said.

"Can I see Jean?"

"Why not? Leave the umbrella out here and come on in."

Skip followed him. She was actually inside Jean's house. So often she had wondered what it would be like because Jean never had anyone over. None of the other girls had ever been inside either. It hadn't even occurred to Skip to question this. And now here she was and too nervous to look around.

There was a close smell in the house as if windows should be opened and the place aired. She passed the living room without a glance. She had peered in one day and thought it must be wonderful because Jean was. Now it was only a dark space to her, like passing a hole. The kitchen was in the back of the house and that was where the brother led her.

"Jeannie," he called up the enclosed stairwell. "Move it!" He didn't bother to tell her Skip was there.

It was a large old kitchen with exposed pipes running along the high green ceiling. Every surface had things on it, stove, sink, the top of the refrigerator, counter tops, even the wooden cupboard next to her had two used coffee cups on the narrow ledge. The kitchen smelled of bacon and toast and also something else underneath it all, something rotten.

A bald old man in an undershirt was reading a newspaper at a built-in breakfast nook. He was following the words with his finger, his mouth moving as he read. He didn't look up when they came in.

Skip waited for Jean to come down, certain that the two men could hear her heart thumping away. Sweat gathered under her arms.

A clatter of feet on the steps and there was Jean Persico, wearing the same old diamond-print play dress. A blue seersucker suit jacket was folded over her arms. What Skip noticed first was the locket around Jean's neck.

The brother took away his jacket as Jean stared with hostile surprise at Skip.

"Hey, look who's here." A hint of fear was in the greeting. She flicked her eyes at her brother which made Skip say to her "Don't worry." Jean thought she was here to tell on her about Kaminsky's garden.

The brother was stooping to gaze at himself in a small round mirror on the wall of the stairwell. The heels of his hands were smoothing the sides of his perfect hair. He was totally absorbed, not listening.

The old man in the breakfast nook growled, "More coffee!"

Jean yelled, "In a minute, Pa."

Her father! Skip had thought he must be her grandfather.

The brother caught Jean's wrist in a grasp that made her wince. He held out the sleeve of his jacket and said to her, "You call this an ironing job? Next time, watch it, willya?" He winked at Skip in a way she didn't like. "She wants to spoil my image." Something squeaked in the back of his throat and she realized he must be laughing because he was showing a lot of those crooked teeth.

Jean Persico cried, "Oh, hey Paulie. I'm sorry. Here, give it to me. I'll do it over, honest I will."

Skip blinked at what she was hearing. She didn't know this girl. This was a different person.

He dropped his sister's arm and waved her away. Skip saw her dodge automatically as his hand passed her by.

"So long, Pop," he shouted. The father looked up from his newspaper. "Paolo," he acknowledged and went back to his paper. He looked up again. "You look like a pimp. You gonna wear that to the garage?"

"My day off, Pop. Party time for little Paulie. Hey kiddo," he said to his sister, "see if you can get that tub clean upstairs, whattaya say? A pig wouldn't take a bath in that. Would you?" He laughed again in that squeaky way.

Skip thought of a rat and tried not to shudder.

This brother's jokes were more scary than the other brother's anger.

She turned to look at Jean, but saw Paolo was about to leave. Skip needed him to stay a bit longer. "Excuse me," she said to him. He paused with a lifted eyebrow.

She took a deep breath and said to Jean straight out, "I want my locket." To Paolo she said, "I have to have it back now," expecting him to back her up.

Jean went wide-eyed. She stepped back with a hand on her heart, shocked to the core. "Are you kidding? You gave it to me. Indian giver! She gave it to me, Paulie. Honest, it's mine."

Skip said, "It was for lend. I told you I would have to have it back sometime and now I do." She too turned to the brother in appeal.

He gave a what-do-I-care shrug. "Yeah? You're breakin' my heart, you two. Keep your nose clean, Jeannie. I'll be home for supper, maybe, maybe not." He was gone.

Jean now turned bold eyes at Skip who so recently was her slave. Her whole manner said, I'm still on top.

Unstoppable, unbeatable Jean. She wasn't going to give over the locket.

Skip was overcome. She had no way to manage this. She had to dig down deep for backbone and found it in the memory of a slap and a rat-laugh.

She looked at Jean Persico with different eyes. She had a mess here at home. Skip saw that now. She was sorry, but that wasn't going to stop her. She thought for an instant of threatening to tell her brother Manny on her, but then in the next breath knew she didn't need to do that.

Stepping closer to Jean she held out her hand. "Give it to me," she said. She meant it and it showed.

Jean's eyes shifted. The boldness faded. With a sense of disbelief Skip watched Jean Persico lift her arms to take the locket off. She had done it! She alone had made Jean do what she wanted. For once she had taken the lead. As if power were an odor, she took a deep shaky breath.

Her exultation carried her to the door and out into the rainy day. She stood on the Persico porch and looked over the street. Gray, deserted, dirty, she loved it. She didn't want to open the umbrella. With the rain pelting her face she began to run across the street to Ellie's house. Maybe Ellie didn't want to be friends anymore, but Skip knew she could change that.

Kaminsky stepped out of the Berman house with his suitcase at that moment, ready to go. He saw the girl running his way with her wet face uplifted, expectant and open to the sky. She reminded him of something, what was it? He began to walk away, and then said to himself, Oh yes, a bud, a flower . . . a rose.

"Come," calls the street. "I have something to show you but you must be quick. An October snap is in the air. The nights grow short and cool. No longer am I the playground. The wild games and running feet are gone, lost to Homework. Soon I will sleep the winter away.

"See there. That's what I want to show you. A bent old woman with a number tattooed on her wrist works in the garden with Kaminsky. They are cutting back the rose bushes, putting them to sleep for the winter along with me. Angela is with them every day after school. She calls the woman Aunt Sophia.

"Skip and Ellie watch."